Slow Guillotine

ZERO STREET FICTION

Series Editors
Timothy Schaffert
SJ Sindu

SLOW GUILLOTINE

A Novel

Teo Rivera-Dundas

University of Nebraska Press | Lincoln

© 2026 by the Board of Regents of the University of Nebraska

The University of Nebraska Press is part of a land-grant institution with campuses and programs on the past, present, and future homelands of the Pawnee, Ponca, Otoe-Missouria, Omaha, Dakota, Lakota, Kaw, Cheyenne, and Arapaho Peoples, as well as those of the relocated Ho-Chunk, Sac and Fox, and Iowa Peoples.

For customers in the EU with safety/GPSR concerns, contact:
gpsr@mare-nostrum.co.uk
Mare Nostrum Group BV
Mauritskade 21D
1091 GC Amsterdam
The Netherlands

Library of Congress Cataloging-in-Publication Data can be found at search.catalog.loc.gov:
ISBN 978-1-4962-4731-5 (paperback)

Designed and set in Garamond Premier Pro by Lacey Losh.

For J

SLOW

OR
WORKING INSIDE THE CUBE
 OR
  IT ONLY GOES IN ONE DIRECTION
   OR
    A BRIGHT BEADLIKE ROW OF UNAFFILIATED MOMENTS
     OR
      AN EXPERT IN SOMETHING THAT IS UNNECESSARY
       OR
        THE WORLD'S GOT EVERYTHING IN IT
         OR
          THE SITUATION IS MORE DIRE STILL

GUILLOTINE

Ten Notes about Work before We Can Get Started

1.

Here are the types of packing material: bubble wrap, butcher paper scraps, wiggly cardboard scraps, packing peanuts (blue polystyrene), packing peanuts (biodegradable thermoplastic starch, a corn derivative, edible), and weird bone- or meat-cross-section-looking cardboard chunks. Also there's the filler Hachette Book Group sends with their cookbooks, a solid foam in the perfect negative space shape of whatever was—or wasn't, I guess—in the box. These are uncanny, art object-type pieces, basically useless unless you're prepared to pack an outgoing shipment the exact size and shape of the negative space foam. We throw this (nonbiodegradable, immortal) foam away, and try not to think about it.

Hachette happens to be the least evil of the five big publisher-distributors, apart from their use of hyperobject packing filler. I learn this from Dima. HarperCollins is owned by Rupert Murdoch, Simon and Schuster is Viacom, Penguin Random House is an endlessly consumptive monopoly blob, and Macmillan Publishing Services is some inscrutable British company that Dima tells me has ties to weapons manufacturing. Is this actually true? I don't know.

2.

I really like books. Ford hired me for the receiving room after I told him so. I wanted to work the sales floor, as a regular bookseller, but the back room had an opening and I needed the job. Now I internalize corporate gossip, shipping and receiving jargon—I guess knowing all this can become a kind of skill, or hobby, eventually, too.

3.

Within the packing material, the book. Beyond the receiving room, the bookstore.

4.

Today, it's me and Arthur. Arthur is singing.

I grip the tape roller with both hands. He sings, but his voice has nowhere to land. It rummages through the receiving room and crashes, flailing, onto the floor. I grip the blue plastic handle of the tape roller, which is indented at the fingers, with both hands. The in-progress box I hold between my legs. My feet I plant on the floor, knees buckling against the standing desk.

The sound made by the tape roller as it peels over a cardboard box's two central flaps. The long pull of plastic, then a rip. Arthur shelves the returns. Music plays over his singing. The two songs—one from the speakers above my computer and the other issuing out of Arthur's mouth—have, as far as I can tell, decoupled.

I finish the last box and heave it to the top of its pile. When the next load comes in I'll slice each box open one at a time, keeping it down with my legs. And if Arthur is still singing then I will hold the boxcutter with both hands.

5.

Maybe this is the wrong way to start. I am not actually going to freak out and attack Arthur with a boxcutter or anything. All I mean to say is that my attention looks for something to hold onto, moments like these. Arthur and I share the room. We perform the same two or three tasks for eight hours at a time, unmediated by conversation or any mutual interest in one another. I lift fifty-pound boxes with my back. I take a fifteen-minute break on the curb and return inside. Such conditions produce either trance or obsession. Small things expand. It's a phenomenon I'm tracking, starting now.

The punch clock, the two computers at their standing desks, the point-of-sale and inventory software. Last year's calendar open to next month.

A system of ropes hugs the receiving room ceiling, keeping a mass of trash bags loaded with packing material in declining blobs above us. Every day either I or Arthur or Dima (who's still out) will fill a trash bag with packing material from incoming shipments, hoist the bag into the rope netting zone, and then take it down again a few hours later, using its packing material to stuff outgoing shipments. But because we end up collecting more material than we use, the ceiling is constantly, slowly, lowering.

6.

Ford calls. He needs Arthur downstairs for shelving. "Good," I say, and send him down.

Dima is still out. Yesterday he called from Moscow and told me about a pro-government demonstration that ended in a big roundup of imported cheese being run over by a tank or a bulldozer or something. He said this happened right in the central revolutionary square, people throwing their Western cheese products into a growing pile, and that it was staged as a spontaneous patriotic thing but was in fact a minor government operation meant to foment anti-NATO sentiment. I asked him why cheese, but he just described the way the pile looked after getting steamrolled: *flat brie, listen, flat thin dirty bleu, dirty cheese, but paper cheese . . .*

Dima is the one who taught me about certain packing peanuts being edible. You can also lick them at the ends and stick them together, and because they're weightless you can assemble surprisingly large packing peanut sculptures this way. It's all cornstarch.

7.

Someone has rolled in the day's returns using one of the red handcarts they have out on the sales floor.

Before he left, Dima trained me to file returns. Here's how it works: sort every book by distributor, stacking each title on the shelves labeled PRH or SS or whatever, respectively. Vintage is Penguin, Tor is MPS, New Directions is Norton, Coffee House is Perseus, Anchor is Penguin, Norton is Norton, FSG is MPS, Archipelago is Penguin, Melville House is Penguin, tiny presses are usually SPD, Chicago is Chicago, Columbia is Wiley, Scholastic is Scholastic, Vintage is Penguin again, Graywolf is MPS, Scribner is Simon, Ecco is Harper, Harper is Harper, Knopf is Penguin, Puffin is Penguin, Random House is Penguin, Penguin is Penguin.

These, and a few dozen adult coloring books at the bottom of my handcart. That has to be a mistake—Ford recently implemented a "buy a coloring book get *My Brilliant Friend* half off" special that

became so popular he had to discontinue it. People started returning *My Brilliant Friend* for full store credit just to turn around and
buy another coloring book, essentially for free.

I draw a question mark on a pink Post-it, slap this to the top-
most coloring book, and stack.

8.

Ford is about to walk into the room and say something. I can feel
it. He's about to stride his seven-foot-tall leatherette mass in here
and say *listen we need to think about how we proceed with X or Y
folks it's important*. He'll say *folks* even though he's talking just to
me. Ford's green voice and boat shoes. In his office there are two
books about how to build a yacht, up on a shelf twelve feet off the
ground. Do you build them from scratch or what?

Here he comes. The year is 2014, or it's 2015—it doesn't matter,
either works. Ford crams his massive face into the room. "Milton is
on his way," he says. Then he eyes the coloring books on the return
stack and stoops over, rapping them with his enormous knuckles. "You are not just blithely returning adult coloring books right
now, folks," he says. "We need to *think* about how we work. These
should've been at the registers yesterday."

He looks at the return pile, looks at me looking at him, then
looks at the drooping penis statue Dima made out of licked-together
packing peanuts just before he left. "For God's sake," Ford says.

9.

An hour or so later the intrastore phone rings: Milton's here. I tell
Ford to give me Arthur back, and then I pull the convertible hand
truck from under my standing desk and roll it to the elevator. At the
curb, there's Milton, perched against his double-parked minivan,

smoking. He hands me a cigarette, and a minute later we're hauling boxes from his minivan onto the hand truck.

When I first started, Dima explained the Milton situation. Let's say you knew a guy, call him Philton, who works at one of the major book distribution warehouses. Alright. Say every now and again, maybe every three weeks, a pallet of boxes of books fell off this guy's truck. Well, the distributor who owns the warehouse—especially a distributor major enough to have multiple warehouses, shipping, say, global quantities of science fiction trade paperbacks—well, they barely notice when stock goes missing, or so says Milton, or so says Ford, according to Dima. And if a couple hundred sci-fi paperbacks with titles like *Perihelion Uprising* and *Ninth Fae: A Gereon Ëxter Novel* end up in our return pool, then, well, such an enormous distributor would happily pay us to have these back, this kind of thing happens all the time, and if we make a few thousand dollars on the side returning inventory we never had to buy in the first place, great. By *we*, of course, I mean the store. Milton gets his cut.

It's the least he can do to share his shitty Camels with me as we lift fifty-pound boxes, one after the other, onto a small mountain on the hand truck.

When we finish, Milton asks if I've met any special ladies in the Big Apple. I tell him I have, and that I am in love. Then Milton does a thing where he looks at me, adjusts his crotch, says *alright then boss*, and drives away.

10.

By the time I've wheeled the boxes past the front registers—past New Releases and milling customers side-eyeing tote bags, into a three-point reversal to fit diagonally in the elevator, up the elevator, past the second floor information desk and buyback booth, past Middle Readers and Young Adult, and into the receiving room—

by the time this is done, Arthur has cleared an area for me by the standing desks and waits with his arms out for the boxes. I heave them at him, lifting with my back. He catches and stacks.

I plant my feet on the floor and flick open a boxcutter, keeping the first box in place with my legs as I slice it open. The bubble wrap I tear from the box and stuff into an in-progress trash bag, which quickly fills. I toss the bag to Arthur, who hoists it into the netting zone above us. The ceiling lowers. Each book has to be individually scanned into the point-of-sale and inventory software, which, because these are Milton-ass sci-fi trade paperbacks, the majority of them don't show up in the store's system and we have to do data input manually. The process takes forever and is why, before he left to visit his dad in Moscow, Dima changed the receiving room computers' passwords to *fuckmilton*. I boot mine up and put on the song of the summer, which is twenty minutes long and will forever represent my moving to the Big Apple and falling in love. Arthur, who has never heard this song in his life, begins to sing. Alright then boss. We scan. With everything scanned in, we start the return, which is going to Macmillan Publishing Services. We launder the stolen sci-fi with actual stock from the return shelves. Minotaur is MPS, Forge is MPS, Picador is MPS, Starscape is MPS, Graywolf is MPS, Tor is MPS. Arthur, neck jutting back and forth with the music, pulls a trash bag down from the ceiling and tears out a long bunch of butcher paper. I fill a box, holding it in place with my legs, and Arthur stuffs its negative space with paper. A good box you should be able to stand on no problem, no bowing with your weight or anything like that. I tape the box shut using the tape roller, which is blue plastic, indented at the fingers, a perfect negative space shape for the thin layer of skin holding back my blood, and which I hold with both hands.

Another Note
(to the Reader)

Dear reader: Please imagine that, throughout all the stories I'm about to tell you, everything in the ten notes above is also happening. If you want you can imagine the notes out of order, or in new arrangements—prime numbers only, or beginning in the middle and ping-ponging out in both directions. Or imagine an endless loop, one through ten, one through ten, forever. Receiving, lifting, stacking. It doesn't matter. The content of those scenes plays and replays behind the other things that happen, like a car alarm.

Another way of saying what I want to say might be: Every weekday, from nine to five, I will take a break from the plot of this novel, such as it is, in order to go to work, to have my little work dramas. If I ever seem burnt-out, or stupid, or cranky, that will be one reason why.

Thank you for understanding.

In the Summer We Are Inside Preparing Food

Actually, I do think our building might turn the gas on soon. Precious and I have been fighting about this. He says no way. I think I'm right.

It's not just the endless construction downstairs. There have been memos. Every few weeks, for the past maybe three months, Precious and I have woken up to another memo from the building management company taped to our front door, stating in massive Comic Sans that they're aware of the issue and are closely tracking new developments, like it's a court case or something. Maybe it's the diligence of these memos that has me optimistic.

And then there's the construction. Just this week, the stairwell one floor under ours got a fresh coat of beige paint, along with signs everywhere threatening WET PAIN in the big Comic Sans. And that's just this week.

"I mean, if they weren't working on it," I call to Precious from the kitchen, biting into a bagel he made from scratch, "why take the time to write so many memos?" And why then tape each memo to the doors of every inhabited unit, six floors all the way up?

Yesterday Precious told me he saw a new memo, this one affixed to the building's front door with some kind of official-seeming saran wrap tape. "From the city," he said, and according to this latest memo the gas was turned off because its piping was never permitted in the first place, something about the amount of piping per square foot or the density of the pipes themselves, and that either way the city shut it off over a year ago, before we moved in. Precious told me this as though he was winning some argument.

The city's memo was gone by the time I got home from the bookstore; I never saw it.

"And what about the construction?" I said. "They're going crazy down there."

He said the memo also mentioned something about how our landlords had failed to make payments to the city for several years, and there was a section about what we as tenants were entitled to given that the lack of gas wasn't our fault, but he didn't completely understand this part and forgot to take a picture of it, and anyway his hands were full of groceries.

"What do you think of the bagels," says Precious now, wandering into the kitchen, chewing. "Kind of doughy?"

"The construction, though," I say. "The memos."

Final data point. Earlier today someone cut a hole in our hallway ceiling. I didn't see it until Precious pointed it out, but then there it was: a body-sized, papered-over rectangle hovering directly above me. I could feel it in my butt.

"They came right after you left," he said, "and worked for like five hours."

"Doing the gas?"

"Maybe, I don't know," said Precious, "because look, they cut another hole in the kitchen." He pawed for his phone and held it up to me, playing a blue video of a couple workers sawing into and then papering over our ceiling. "I think they have to give us at least a day's warning."

Back and forth, back and forth. "I like the bagels," I say now.

"But you're making rice."

I am making rice. I measure a cup of rice to a cup and a half of water and pour both into a pot. The pot goes on the hot plate we found in the dumpsters behind our building. Only one of the hot plate's burner coils works, and it's small, and it takes much longer than the stove to my immediate left would to cook anything, but it was free. Precious and I have outfitted our entire kitchen through dumpsters—the standard microwave, but also a toaster oven, an electric kettle, a plug-in panini press. People will throw away fully functional machines, I learn, or basically functional. It's like a magic trick.

The water in the pot on the hot plate considers its composition but fails to boil. My dream is for someone in our neighborhood to throw out a rice cooker. Hopefully this happens soon.

Precious flings his big body onto our tiny couch. I hear the sound of fifteen-second videos.

Our kitchen window looks directly into our neighbor's kitchen, which is probably twenty feet away but in a separate building from ours, a whole other microcosm. A long, buttery light fills this other kitchen, which seems to have been laid out as a mirror version of our own. There's a black cat on the mirror stove, staring back at me, or staring into its own window reflection. Otherwise the room is empty. Precious and I have watched the person who lives in this apartment across the gap smoke on his fire escape, and we've heard him scream on the phone and listen to Radiohead at weird hours, and we've seen him walk naked through his kitchen a few times, but neither of us have ever seen him cook, not once.

◻ ◻ ◻

The day we signed the lease, I crushed my phone hoisting Precious's massive backpack onto my knee. The phone was in my pocket, and I could feel rather than hear the crunch of its green glass on my thigh as a corner of the backpack dug in. An omen, it felt like—something auspicious. At the time I busied myself looking for signals such as these.

The day we moved in, we brought my duffel bag of books, Precious's backpack, the old man's rug, and a mattress Precious found at an estate sale somewhere in Westchester, which almost flew off the roof of his RAV4 after we hit sixty on the Hudson River Parkway. That became my bed. Then there was the sleeping bag Precious produced from his backpack, his bed, replaced after a couple weeks by a mattress we found in the back of a ninety-nine cents store—it cost a hundred dollars—and carried down 125th Street and up into our apartment, trying but failing to ensure that it never touched the ground. It was drizzling that day. That felt auspicious too.

I say duffel bag full of books, but really it was just *An African in Greenland* by Tété-Michel Kpomassie, which I had purchased at random, and an old copy of *Capitalism and Schizophrenia*, which I took from some dead Columbia professor's apartment after clearing it out. This took a full shift and ended with me wheeling a collapsing hand truck of boxes of this professor's books back to the shop so Ford could appraise it for resalable stock. *This person wanted their belongings donated to a store*, was all I could think, trying to understand Deleuze on the train. The rest of the duffel bag was full of normal things, shirts and toothpaste and whatever else.

So it was for a while. I would go to work and Precious would go to school and we would return home at the exact same time, having taken different cars on the same uptown train. One of us would open the door to our unit and we'd see the old man's beautiful rug in the common room, my mattress in my room and Precious's in his, and that was it. In those early days I sat on the roof of our building and read, while Precious watched videos of old people in dark rooms doing the latest dance or lip syncing over the most recent outrageous news clip or just saying deranged shit with the whites of their eyes glistening in the light of their own phones. He texted me his favorites, though I could never actually see what was happening through the spiderweb of my phone's cracked screen.

Precious, an artist, came to New York because he wanted to make videos of his own. He wanted somehow to document everyday moments in a way that elaborated on their absurdity, and do this in such a way that other people would instinctively understand what they were seeing, an odd rippling feeling right under the first layer of skin, even if they didn't entirely *consciously know* what they were looking at. I'm probably getting this wrong. Later it turned out that he also wanted to cook, so he enrolled in one of the culinary schools downtown.

I came to New York because I wanted to live in the city where books happened to be made. I had no theory of power, or of history. Now it's now.

One day Precious found an interesting chair in front of an austere-looking building and brought it in. I found a couple of shipping pallets the exact shape and size of our mattresses and now we use these as bed frames. Precious found a ceramic tiger sticking halfway out of a dumpster downtown, and I found a bunch of plastic roses that fit perfectly in the tiger's open mouth. He bought a TV from the same ninety-nine cents store that sold him his mattress, and I bought several yards of Christmas lights. The view from our front door filled: our beds, our chair, our tiger chewing flowers.

The day we went to IKEA to get everything else, Precious's car had just been towed for the first time. We walked to his special parking spot next to Ulysses S. Grant's tomb and it just wasn't there.

Here's how this works. When your car is towed, you look it up by license plate number on the New York City Department of

Finance Towed Vehicle Locator website, and then you go down to the docks and wait half an hour to pay two hundred dollars to get it back. In the waiting room we composed an illustrated list of IKEA furniture that needed buying, shifting around in our yellow plastic seats: a bookshelf, a couple desks, a table for the common room, chairs, the smallest possible couch we could find, a lamp, kitchen stuff, and a multipurpose storage unit for the kitchen to hold all the stuff. I tried drawing the couch from an acute angle, to emphasize its concision, but couldn't get the perspective right, allowing the drawing to grow into a lopsided mess of curves. We riffed on this sketch for the half hour it took the city to process us—and then we observed a braid of clouds untangle over New Jersey as we slipped past the big aircraft carrier looming over the parkway. Crossing the George Washington Bridge we talked about what would happen if a volcano suddenly burst from the exact center of Central Park. At IKEA we tried consulting our shopping list, but it had become a dumb, hopeless knot.

We bought a bookshelf, a couple desks, a table for the common room, some chairs, the smallest possible couch we could find, a lamp, several plants, a couple soft serve ice creams from the cafeteria, and a wooden rolling storage thing for the kitchen. Altogether, this cost two hundred dollars each—the most I had ever spent in one sitting, aside from rent. We spent too long rolling around the model bedrooms, apparently afflicted with what Precious called *clammer's madness*, though he wouldn't elaborate on what this means. We carried the many boxes up the six flights of stairs into our unit and set it all out in a circle around a half-empty bottle of Maker's Mark. We found ourselves unable to devise any kind of drinking game out of building furniture. By the time Felix came over—I have failed to introduce Felix, but here she comes, bottle of wine under her arm, smelling vaguely of snuffed candles—Precious and I had already made some intractable error assembling the tiny couch and were working to forgive its pathetic declining slump.

"How many other IKEA couches have this much personality right out of the box," I said.

"You're spilling whiskey on it," said Precious. "What's the damn rush?"

Felix poured herself a thumb of Maker's Mark and sat on my bed with *An African in Greenland*, and then she fell asleep with the book tented over her face. I said if a volcano erupted in the middle of Central Park at this exact moment the important thing is that those skinny skyscrapers that look like cell phone slices would explode. "Those would be the first to go," I said. "They'd find skyscraper chunks near the IKEA. People would actually get a chance inspect them at eye level."

"If a volcano erupted right now," said Precious, "then we'd know how many of the people who live in those things have private helicopters. The buildings would still blow up, but the billionaires would manage to fly out of there at the last minute. They'd have known in advance somehow."

"No one even lives in those buildings," said Felix from my bedroom, awake and propped on an elbow. "They pay an obscene amount to visit, and they have their parties, they take pictures, and then they go back to wherever they came from. Wherever billionaires actually live."

□ □ □

The gas stays off. The old man calls asking about it. "Still off," I say, "but I do think the building people are fixing it soon." We've had this conversation numerous times, and every time I have to explain that the gas being off doesn't mean the heat doesn't work. The heat isn't good either—when I tested the radiator in my bedroom it sneezed a scalding liquid from a nozzle that I think must be missing a knob to plug it shut, so I dammed the whole apparatus with a towel, which has since started to disintegrate: a dripping, biological mass of warm dewy cloth. But the heat does work. The shower works. Those are separate systems from cooking gas.

"Fine," says the old man. "But what is your backup plan when it starts getting cold? Where are you going for showers?"

"I just told you," I say.

He expresses care via interrogation. "Have you talked to your neighbors?" he asks. "Have you tried calling the city? What would happen if you withheld rent? Who is this bastard your landlord anyhow? What does it say in your lease, exactly? Isn't your roommate a cook? Is he upset he can't cook in his own home? Or is it kind of a vacation for him? Does he eat at work? Does he ever bring anything back for you? What was that restaurant we went to when I visited? Does your roommate work there? And what about your job? Have you started looking for something better? What? What?"

The apartments across the street look empty. It looks like they're waiting to be demolished. Are they?

"I met someone recently," I tell the old man. Precious emerges from the bathroom in a rush of steam and a clay face mask.

"No," I say, "someone new. Her name is Felix."

Precious mouths *Is it Gramps* and gestures toward his baggie of weekend-ritual weed. I nod my head yes, then shake my head no thank you.

"Well, that's her name," I say. "It does mean happy. Anyone can be named happy, I'm pretty sure." Precious rolls himself a joint and clambers out to the fire escape, touching his face.

"Not Felicia," I say. "Not Felicity. It's Felix. Listen, old man. Listen. It's Felix."

□ □ □

Felix on the train, Felix on the front stoop of her building, Felix sneaking past Ford into the receiving room as my shift ends. She shows me where to buy the really enormous plantains and we make tostones for Precious, who has never had them, and who won't stop calling them *banana taters*. Felix in a room packed with other people, talking to everyone. Strangers complimenting Felix's dancing, strangers who want to photograph Felix for online street-fashion purposes, strangers on the train who can't help but make some comment. A sunny room full of almond pastries and amaretto-spiked coffee and Felix.

And then also, throughout everything, the song of the summer: in the train or floating through the air above me and bouncing off all the empty buildings. One of her many bosses flies to London for the weekend and asks Felix to cat sit, but when we get there the apartment is excruciatingly hot and reeks of cats. Felix with an assembly of essential oils and lemon soap, sweating, scrubbing the wood floors. "Excelsior," she says. We buy dollar slices from the pizza place next door and dress them up with basil and arugula, tomatoes that have a taste and eggplants shaped like eggs, whatever high-powered produce we can find in her boss's fridge. The cats stare at us. "Maybe everything is edible," says Felix in a box of sunlight, chewing.

□ □ □

It may not surprise you to learn that we are new in this city. Felix has been here longest, knows the most, but that's still only a matter of months.

I learn the importance of developing a routine and slotting into it. And whether I realize it or not, over time I develop a second layer of skin, but one stretched over the city as a whole, so that brushing up against it becomes contact with another version of myself.

For example: I get home from the bookstore, eat whatever Precious has brought back from school, and then fall asleep without meaning to—half naked on the couch, fully clothed in bed, mid-conversation, book between my legs—a blank, dreamless sleep that lasts from eight or nine until usually around eleven at night. Part of the routine involves a dependable feeling of shock when I wake up. I look at my phone and fail to understand the time, sitting there. Precious by this point will have closed his bedroom door for the night.

I take the train downtown to meet Felix at her job at the art gallery, which becomes a nightclub-type performance art space after a certain hour. I sit in the glassed-off break room behind a makeshift catwalk with exactly enough light to read by until she's able to clock off and we can get a drink or some samosas and head back uptown. The subway turns local after a certain hour, and waiting with Felix in the Broadway-Lafayette station, sitting on the train as it opens its doors and half closes them and opens them again, occupying the low murmur between sentences, all this allows time to slip and slip and slip.

Here's my project. Here's what I do. I take notes on our jobs. My job, Felix's job, Precious's. I keep a filing cabinet with various folders. The folders refer to one another. I zero in on details. If I do this enough then maybe I will understand something about work. What is work? What are our days for?

Here's how it is with Felix. During the day she attends to the regular needs of an art gallery, sitting behind the white semicircular desk at the end of a glass-and-concrete room. She responds to queries from buyers and agencies, pitches upcoming shows to magazines, schedules her bosses' reiki and acupuncture appointments. She processes the various shipping logistics that arise from the gallery's need to, say, transport a twelve-foot painting from a studio in the Bronx to an art fair in Miami: obtaining a custom-fitting wood pallet, and custom-fitting foam insulation to line it, and movers with special training to handle it, and special climate-controlled precious cargo shipping conditions both in the immediate term (Bronx to the airport) and beyond (the plane to Miami, then that airport to the art fair) to transport, unpack, and eventually hang the painting inside it. She does all this in absolute silence, punctuated by the gallery's glass doors opening and closing with the arrival of a stray civilian. The whoosh of traffic outside and then silence again.

The gallery vacillates back and forth between exhibiting featureless, hotel-ready abstract paintings and multimedia art pieces in active dialogue with political events from several decades ago. Images of prisoners from Abu Ghraib projected onto a monumental clay slab. Meticulously rendered recreations of old Disney shorts but with Lenin and Mao substituted in for Mickey and Pluto. A room full of plastic bins containing crickets, corn syrup, palm oil, bleached flour. Felix clicks at her desk. The neighborhood is lousy with bars.

Some nights the gallery transforms into a performance space, meaning Felix will work a twelve- to fourteen-hour shift a few days out of every week.

Tonight, for example: On this very night, the gallery hosts a black-tie election fundraiser for a prominent centrist city council member at risk of losing her seat to a budding, internet-famous fascist. "These," says Felix, shrugging, "we host these kinds of thing too." She smells like gasoline and wasabi, and offers me a piece of salmon from a glass plate. "Find me in a couple hours," she says, "hopefully it won't be too long a night."

My body sings its work song. Since starting in the receiving room and lifting boxes with my back for eight hours each day, it has become difficult for me to sit on any comfortable surface without immediately falling asleep. But when Felix works nights it's important for me to stay awake, or to time my sleep carefully between periods of getting to see her. The gallery's spinning leather chairs are deep enough to sink into—and when I wake up, the house lights have come on and the audience shuffles away.

The uptown train has probably turned local. If I were to look for Felix now I would find her slipping from room to room, murmuring into a walkie talkie, putting out fires. In twenty minutes she'll return to her small office, the one behind frosted glass walls, where I'm sitting now. She'll crouch over her desk with a bottle of wine in order to input archival data for the gallery's internal use. Then she'll be ready. The neighborhood's bars will still be open.

□ □ □

Dear reader: I'm going to be as upfront as possible. There's something to these hours, which accrete into whole days. There's value to them, to their details, or at least the ones I notice. Connections are made, connections fail to be made. And then, behind that, there's the network of details I fail to notice, a language of unarticulated signals, another person's gestures, or the tone of their voice, or the bags under Felix's eyes as she emerges from her small office behind the main gallery and into the night. These, too, are there, transmitting meaning in ways I am not a deft enough person to see, let alone capture. What I can put down, though, what happens in these moments I present to you now as scenes—something constellates out of them. I'm pretty sure. We go to work, we come home. You'll forgive me for being so direct about this.

□ □ □

The rest of the summer we spend eating and sleeping, gathering furniture.

Two hours ago, Precious unsheathed his licensed replica of Glamdring, Gandalf's sword, and told me he was ordering takeout from the ramen place down the block. Half an hour later we were watching the prologue battle of the first *Lord of the Rings*, Precious at the table carefully mixing one of his homemade hot sauces into the ramen's broth, me at the foot of the couch already beginning to fall asleep.

Now we're both on the couch, Glamdring spread over our knees like a blanket. Gandalf can't figure out the password to get into the Mines of Moria. If I fall asleep, I'll miss Felix's call, which, if I don't miss it, could lead to her coming over in an hour or two, around midnight. We'll have finished the movie by then, or Precious will have queued up *The Two Towers* and we'll be midway through another opening sequence: Gandalf's big showdown with the Balrog, who appears for the first time a few minutes from now, after the octopus monster and the cave troll and all the orcs.

The papered-over hole in the hallway ceiling makes a sudden flap. I jump awake, linking the sound to the octopus monster grasping Frodo's ankles, and this jolts Precious, who laughs. "It's been so loud today," he says, reaching for the remote. "I think it's picking up a draft inside the walls." The hole makes its sound again, a stronger whip this time, paper bowing and pushing. Frodo and Gandalf run from the monster, and a rockslide at their heels builds into an avalanche that caves the fellowship inside the face of the mine. "It's one thing after another," Precious says.

Construction workers came into our unit earlier today to do something in the common room, but Precious didn't find out what. He let them in and then retreated to his bedroom—and then a few hours passed before he realized they were still there, drilling and sawing, and that he'd unconsciously tuned out the sound. "When I opened the door all I could see was one of the guy's legs on a ladder, disappearing into the ceiling hole. I recorded it, look." On his phone, the still image of one ladder, two legs, and the square hole, in that order, ascending. Then comes the sound of muffled singing—not photo but video, I realize—and a rapid zoom on the hole until it overtakes the whole screen. "It's gotten a couple thousand views already," says Precious. "Which is funny, because nothing happens. There's no punchline."

"You hid in your room for hours like that?" I ask. "Filming?"

Gandalf says something to the effect of *this mine is way haunted*.

"I think they forgot I had let them in," he says. "You know. I didn't want to surprise them."

The ceiling hole makes its paper sound again, and I jump again.

Precious's videos periodically become famous, though he never does. The more successful ones seem almost to drift away from him, becoming ubiquitous and without definite origin over time, more a common language than created things. Maybe this is just how it works online. One video—thirteen seconds of me naked and wrapped in Precious's West Virginia flag drunkenly mixing up the words to "Take Me Home, Country Roads" and then projectile vomiting at his phone—made *me* famous, kids for weeks shooting glances in my direction on the train. But then the video spawned copycats, and a whole micro-genre of naked kids wrapped in different flags shouting or screaming various catchphrases at the camera started cropping up, and everyone more or less forgot about the original.

I think Precious is still trying to link his weird, anonymous success posting videos online with the rest of his life. He is trying, in my opinion, to render his own life explicable, exactly in its chance and unsteadiness, maybe first of all to himself. That's one theory.

The Balrog lashes at Gandalf with its lava whip. Precious walks over to the papered-over ceiling hole, brandishing Glamdring. Frodo wails. The tip of the sword pushes against the taut brown paper. My phone vibrates. "Film me," Precious says, and stabs.

A Snake Appearing
in Dreams

I am slowly learning the broader connective system of small-scale bookselling economics. Here's what happens. In this economy, the bookstore purchases new stock (books) at a discount of 35–46 percent directly from publishers, who are also sometimes distributors, which is different in terms of the means of production, though that's not really important. The books are received by me or Dima or Arthur into the store's point-of-sale and inventory software. The store attempts to sell the books. But then, inevitably, the majority of new books don't sell. Fiction in translation. A debut on a small press. Every few weeks Ford compiles a list of non-sellers, and these are taken off the shelves and rolled into the receiving room on one of the red handcarts, then returned by me or Arthur or Dima back to the publisher-distributor for credit. The books then live in one of the publisher-distributor's many warehouses, from which point they are either resold to some other bookstore, or they languish like that for months, possibly years, taking up space in the warehouse, until they're pulped.

Pulped, that's the official word. I imagine someone training a hose on an endless line of unwanted books as they pass through an industrial shredder, the way workers hose down demolition sites so they don't burst into flames. The process I imagine ends in massive cubes of wet pulp congealing on the warehouse lot, ready to be smeared into new forms. Books transforming into shopping bags—or the cardboard boxes we use to send more books off to be pulped.

I didn't know any of this stuff until recently. Dima helps fill gaps. For example: The business Ford conducts with the publisher-distributors happens entirely on credit, and when the credit line dips below zero, the publisher-distributors freeze the store's accounts because there's no money actually there. Or: When a new book comes out in paperback, we return the first edition hardcover stock of that particular title to the distributor, who will immediately pulp these editions or else sell them en masse to certain other, middleman-type publisher-distributors, who resell hardcover editions at a significantly reduced rate, as remainder copies, to still other bookstores. *Remainders*, that's another official word, meaning newish books no one wanted at full price. They usually have a red dot or dash on the bottom edge of their binding. You may own a few of these, reader. On the sales floor, remainders can be found strewn about the customer's feet, planted in little stacks, pleading.

Sometimes a book or whole boxes of books will show up damaged. When this happens Dima or I call the publisher-distributor, or rather the distributor's call center, which is always either in Georgia or one of the Dakotas. The women—universally women—at the call centers are extremely patient. They tell us to *please destroy the damaged copy*, and that's another word, *destroy*. Destruction of damaged stock happens on the honor system. Nobody calls to follow up about it. Then they send a replacement shipment over, for free. It's a magic trick. I start to have an idea.

Certain books have special return exceptions. When we return mass market paperbacks—books the shape of a small brick, airport thrillers or cheap romance or Stephen King novels—we're told to rip the front cover off and throw the book itself away. No, sorry, *destroy* it. On the inside cover of these kinds of books there's a barcode that we and our proxies at the distributor's warehouse both scan for inventory; this is all they need. My idea starts to grow legs. Scrabble dictionaries, annotated Shakespeare, English-to-Spanish phrase books, *Dune*, Dostoevsky but never Tolstoy, *The Hobbit* but never Harry Potter, Kafka, *The Autobiography of Malcolm X*, and various books from Milton's minivan, a wide host of almost impressively anonymous fantasy.

Then there are used books. On the second floor, right by the receiving room, there is a buyback table where customers can bring in their old Faulkner or Ottolenghi for cash or store credit. With used books, Ford likes to pull a scam similar to the Milton thing: If secondhand stock doesn't sell after a few months, he tells us to return it to the distributor, even when the books are way out of print, even if it's obvious he never bought the books new and so it's insane to expect the distributor's reimbursement for our returning them. Still, he usually gets some credit for these. The books just have to be in decent shape. Used returns are guaranteed to be pulped.

One day I learn that someone works in the windowless back office adjacent the buyback table, and that it is this person's job to buy and sell books on Amazon. A hard-to-find book, for example, or a signed copy, will end up on the store's official Amazon retailer page, which exists. Or if a customer wants something out of print, something we can't obtain through the approved channels, it's this person's job to buy it on Amazon for three dollars or whatever and then sell it for nine or ten. On the stairway of the sales floor, above the pleading stacks of remainders, we sell tote bags screen-printed with slogans about the continued importance of supporting independent bookstores in the face of Amazon's market hegemony.

All this allows me to feel nothing when I begin stealing books from the receiving room. It starts slowly, with damaged stock and coverless trade paperbacks, which would have gone in the trash anyway—nineteenth-century novels I'm embarrassed not to have already read, but also a Spanish-English dictionary, Octavia Butler. That's enough for a couple weeks. Then Ford has a new hire clear out a shelf's worth of Philosophy & Religion in order to make room for more copies of *The God Delusion*, and I find myself stacking old editions of *The Cloud of Unknowing* and *The Six Enneads* and *The Complete Works of Sor Juana Inés de la Cruz* on a shelf in the top corner of the standing desk behind my computer, where only I ever go, and which, really, you can only even see from a position that only I ever occupy. Now most Fridays I'll slip one or two books from my secret shelf into my backpack and bring them home.

I probably don't even need to be sneaky about it. It's not like Dima—who has recently discovered English-language rap music and has pinned a photo of a pig wearing a police hat with a red *X* through it onto the wall behind his computer—will tell on me. Over time I think about stealing books as an ongoing act of liberation: from the books getting pulped, from their making any more money for Amazon, from their sitting on a return shelf for thirty years, from their becoming caught in the endless loop of warehouse to bookstore to warehouse.

Today I'm taking *The Interior Castle*. Next week I think I'll expand my pool to include used undamaged fiction, sliding further out to the more remote concentric rings until I end up stealing perfectly new stock and calling the centers in Georgia or the Dakotas saying they came in busted.

"Smoke break," says Dima, as the label machine prints, as the lights flicker and another day bleeds into the next, and out we go.

□ □ □

With Precious it's like this: I call and he immediately picks up with *talk to me*, a hedge fund manager seconds away from stepping into his convertible. In his car, on the way to an import-export-type supermarket in Queens, he selects a CD from a leather binder that he inherited from his much older half sister, something incomprehensible like Sixpence None the Richer, and we cross the Triborough Bridge while he sings along to "Kiss Me" in his most guttural Appalachian accent, growling when the singer goes high and extending every vowel into diphthong: *kiy-uss may-uh*. With any meal his first bite is accompanied by a pained face, as though the food were intolerably sour; when the meal ends he mimes flipping the table. The weather changes and he says *end of the damn world*. He buys a VHS player so he can assess and eventually digitize the gay porn tapes we find spilling out of a trash bag behind our apartment. These will make it into some video. Then, someone in his family calls, his grandmother, his half sister, and he stares at the name for several seconds before bringing the phone to his ear, opening with *hey* in a small voice. A conversation turns toward feeling, loneliness or the root of some vague anger, and he appends every sentence with *you know*, waving his hand in dismissal.

With Felix it's like this: We have a conversation during a meal and she brings her fork to her mouth, a twirled-up bouquet of pasta, and holds it there until we're both done talking. Then she eats in silence, thinking. Conversation as a whole—or maybe only undeliberate conversation, idle chat, small talk—presents its obstacles. Someone says something she finds baffling or stupid and she responds with *absolutely*, a look of disbelief and a smile. Someone says something cynical or mean and she counters with *excelsior*, but then, she also says this when she means it. She covers her eyes with both hands and pulls her head back until you can see the red below the eyelids. On the phone Felix starts talking without preamble, continuing a conversation that must have been occurring in her head before launching into the next thing. Daily encounters and artifacts are nicknamed: Her gallery becomes *the cube*, her apartment *the garden*, the process of making art *digging*, the act of going to work *debasing myself*, sleeping *rendering*. She finds herself in the middle of an art project that seems to go nowhere and she says something like *feeling the years* or *this shit only goes in one direction*. In this way she is like Precious. Sometimes during a conversation she repeats the last word I've said, or I repeat the last word she's said, holding it in my mouth, worrying it. Or someone says something that seems to jolt her into herself, reminding her of the fact that she lives and will die, and a look mixing fear and ecstasy passes over her face, widening the eyes and flaring her nostrils, until she responds with a rapid, seething *fuck off*.

"Imagine the earth with no oceans," says Precious. "What does it look like? And no lakes or rivers either."

"What about the ice caps?" says Felix.

"Ice caps can stay. And especially the ice shelves, especially, you know, Greenland. But no oceans, no water. Imagine the earth hollowed out to its real shape, something other than a sphere. What does it look like?"

"Like a skull," I say.

"Like a dried up piece of fruit, an apple maybe," says Felix.

"Wrong," says Precious. "Wrong, wrong." But he doesn't tell us the answer.

□ □ □

It gets harder to leave the house.

Not because I'm depressed, nothing like that, but because of the construction. I have to skip down the stairs two at a time to avoid tripping on power tools, wood planks resting at odd angles, buckets full of screws, hammers. Precious devises a method of holding onto the railing with both hands and leaping from the top of a given landing, swinging himself over the stairs six at a time and dropping at a canter onto the next landing. Watching him do this brings back an overwhelming feeling from childhood but nothing like a legible memory.

We agree that the building's lobby has become particularly intense. It's how we mark time. In October, we find the glass front door perpetually wedged open, dozens of people coming and going regardless of the time of day. Every so often I'll spot the building's realtor, Jordan, showing one of the in-progress units to a new group, ignoring me as he passes. He tells the group that the construction will almost definitely be finished by the time their lease begins, which is what he told me. Realtor fee, first month's rent, security deposit, renter's insurance, utilities. I have to add an extra five minutes to my commute time just to exit our apartment, get onto the street, then ten minutes, wriggling against the current through crowds of future tenants, construction workers, and unidentifiable city bureaucrat-looking people milling around with clipboards, fifteen minutes, twenty, tiptoeing over cans of soda and beer, halal cart lunches left half-eaten in open styrofoam containers, slabs of wood in the process of being sawed in half, jackhammer-type chunks of heavy machinery in various states of collapse atop rubble, blue tiles and white grout and a small gray cement mixer, hardhats and yellow construction tape and the splintery raw-and-red-painted wood they use for construction scaffolding. *The entire city is in our building*, I text Felix. I'm exaggerating, of course, but only some.

□ □ □

Something else: It's getting darker earlier. I mean this only as statement of fact. At exactly five my phone buzzes. Ford walks into the receiving room, eyes Dima and me for a few seconds, and walks back out. The lights flicker. "Five," I say.

"Don't go yet," says Dima. "Help me pack this load first." He's playing *Illmatic* on repeat and occasionally breaking into verse, struggling to stay on tempo. "Understandable smooth shit," he says too late. I can hear Arthur singing somewhere on the sales floor. Possibly I imagine this.

"It's getting darker earlier," I say, wedging books into a box four at a time and punching packing material into the negative space between them.

"Russia," says Dima. "New York is becoming one miniature Russia. Happens every winter." I tape the box shut and throw it to the top of the stack. My phone buzzes again, teetering off the edge of my standing desk. "It's okay," Dima says, filing a cigarette behind his ear, "go, I can finish." Then something in the room's air shifts and we both turn to look at the door, as though Ford were about to enter the room again, though he doesn't.

"You need to see this with your own eyes," says Felix on the phone as I walk into the rain. "Are you out?"

"Out," I say. "It's getting darker earlier. Have you noticed?"

"Come over," she says. "I accidentally bought a snake." A garbage truck staggers down Broadway, casting rainwater toward the curb. I jump, though the truck is nowhere near me, and instinctively check my pants to see if they're soaking wet, which they're not. "Are you there?"

"What kind of snake," I say. "You like snakes? I'm getting on the train now."

"I've been thinking about getting one for a while, it's just that today I found myself in an *exotic pet store*," she says these last words in a kind of British accent, "and there she was. Staring at me. They had this parrot at the store too, which flew on my shoulder right when I walked in. It tried eating my ear. You would like it."

"So but," I say. My metro card takes several swipes before I can push through the turnstile.

"There was a litter of baby snakes, all coiling around each other.

They let me hold one. She's so small she slipped into my pocket. I was freaked out and excited and I got an Uber to drive us back to my apartment. I downloaded Uber to do that. That's the story. Are you close?"

"I'm close," I say, as the train pulls in.

It's my first fall season in the Big Apple. I don't understand how anything works. The phone cuts out as we barrel underground. *Be there soon*, I text.

□ □ □

Lately I've been reading books that end with floating, rather than a conclusion. Allow me to explain. These books tend to start normally, taking the time to slot together their various characters, puzzle-piecing a legible enough sense of place and time. From there, they proceed to feed these elements through the book's big narrative machine. Sometimes, often, you can see the wood scaffolding behind the machine itself, as it churns along. You can hear the wood groan, the gears creak. Then, sooner or later, with this kind of book, it becomes obvious that the many elements are doomed to collide, the shitshow keeps ramping up, the machine makes louder and higher-pitched sounds as it churns more plot through the opening slot and out the other side. The dance of near-misses and misheard conversations, various breakdowns, tension, rising action. But then, finally, when those elements seem like they're moments away from crashing into each other—here, at the site of collision, every piece careening hopelessly toward the other—right at that moment a hand comes in from out of view and turns a dial on the valve that controls gravity, and instead of crashing, everything lifts up and out. Slow motion, the room of the scene. Characters, images, themes clonk together and disperse. Floating, hanging together in near-stillness. The hand at the valve holds.

We, reading, can move around this suspended tableau. We can take in the full view of what would have certainly been a calamity. We can absorb every detail from multiple vantage points, stand there staring as you would in a museum.

This, right here, is where the book will end.

I don't know what to do with these endings, but I'm noticing them more and more.

◻ ◻ ◻

Felix's bedroom is full of half-destroyed shit she found on the street. The torso part of a mannequin, a ceramic lamp with no shade, the harp part of a piano, a beautiful dark wood desk with the drawers missing. It's *all* beautiful, actually, the room, the apartment. I don't know how she does it.

"Look," she says, pointing to the stirring corner of fluff in a glass cube on the floor. "Look at that thing in there." We sit on our knees, breathing on the glass. For a long time nothing happens. Fluff moves around. "I'm thinking of giving her my shirt," Felix says, "so she gets used to my smell. They told me at the store I needed the terrarium, and a water dish, and the substrate, which it says on the bag is aspen. Aspen shavings. She still needs a house. A dwelling. Maybe my shirt could be a good dwelling, what do you think?" She doesn't notice, but while Felix talks a tiny orange head emerges from under the aspen fluff and stares at us. It is a snake, but it is also basically a cartoon. "Oh my god," Felix says, finally seeing. "Look. Look at that thing."

◻ ◻ ◻

Really, though, these days I barely read anything at all. The books I take home I tend to convince myself are unreadable. No one has actually cover to cover finished a Beckett novel, for example. Have they? How does *Molloy* end? Is there a living person, reader, who could tell me?

A book of short stories that demands the magazine treatment: flip to any page, scan a few sentences, put it down again. Doing the same for essays, poetry, any kind of anthology. Best new hunter-gatherer writing 1998. The new books with the same cursive font you see on life-affirming coffee mugs designed for colorful still lifes online. Soft revisionist histories about imperialists, war criminals, union busters, slavers. The dead professor's copy of *Capitalism and Schizophrenia* sends me down a confused spiral looking for books like it. Translated monographs describing the radical poet-terrorist, cannibal phenomenology, the musical notation of ecological collapse. These I read on the train. Still, though, and again, maybe *reading* isn't the right word. I steep in them. I find myself caught on a sentence or phrase, rereading it again and again while people shuffle onto and off the train. I try mouthing the words as though I'm learning a new language. *Phe-nom-e-no-log-i-cal.* These books I want to insert into my mouth, and sometimes I do when I'm not thinking, staring out the window as the 1 train peals itself up from underground.

At home, instead of reading, I watch *The Sopranos* with Precious. This week he's learning challah at culinary school and brings home a new braid every day. We eat challah and hummus, challah and salsa, challah and an impromptu bean dip that is just a can of black beans, garlic, salt, lemon, and olive oil all blended together. "This is basically also hummus," Precious says, holding a wedge of challah thick with black bean dip between his thumb and forefinger and shaking his hand at me like Paulie from *The Sopranos*, pinky out.

In today's episode Paulie and Christopher wander around a snowbank after unsuccessfully murdering someone. I try my best to stay awake but end up drooling into my clavicle, half-dreaming about my boxcutter.

□ □ □

Felix lowers Girlfriend into a paper bag and dangles a dead, defrosted mouse above her head, tail between the forefinger and thumb. For a few seconds all Girlfriend does is stare at it, rising slowly on her neck—but then she snaps, clearing the mouse's head in one gesture and collapsing its middle into a corner of the bag. She doesn't seem to swallow so much as twist herself around the mouse's body, going into and back out of knots until the pink fleshy thing disappears.

At the back legs, though, Girlfriend hits some kind of snag and starts to retch. A corner of the mouse spills red back out of her. Now she's mashing her head into her own side trying to get it down. "Sick," says Felix, "oh no." Now Girlfriend's completely still. She pivots, eyes to the ceiling. The mouse wedges through, a passing lump at her neck, her head deflating to its regular size.

The mouse's pink tail disappears in one liquid stroke. Girlfriend's tongue flits. Felix named her Girlfriend. She looks up from the paper bag. What does she see? Two backlit humans peering down.

◻ ◻ ◻

At the culinary school's public-facing restaurant, Precious has to wear white pants, a white collarless button-down shirt, a white apron, and a little white hat. He waits tables every few days, fulfilling some work-study obligation for his financial aid, or meeting the requirements for a unit on hospitality, I can't tell which.

Felix and I decide to visit. White tablecloth, white folded cloth napkins, and a white carafe of ice water with a long sprig of rosemary sticking out of it at every table. White people. We're seated and food starts appearing in front of us. "This is how I get my hair cut, too," says Felix, as a server brings over a tiny bowl of calamari. "Beauty school students will post ads when they're doing free haircuts. The catch is that you have to let them do it however they want.

Sometimes they're amazing." I look at her head, which is completely shaven. "The last one was pretty bad," she says.

When he comes to our table Precious is almost unidentifiable. It's not just the uniform. There's a sanded-off quality to his stare, like the light isn't properly reflecting from his eyes. "Waitstaff," he says. He has snuck over a half-empty bottle of white wine and fills our glasses, the bottle tucked under his sleeve. It looks like wine is flying out of his wrist.

"Are they nice to you here?" asks Felix. I try a piece of calamari; it is easily the best calamari I have ever had. The second piece tastes like a burnt rubber core of pure salt.

"I think this place throws people off," Precious says. "The decor. You expect some fancy thing." He gestures at the room, then manages somehow to pull a flask out of his apron pocket and take a swig from it with the arm that's still holding the concealed bottle of wine. "I think a good percentage of people come here because they want to fuck with us," he says. "They realize we have more to lose if we fight back."

The soup course arrives, and then a pink puzzle piece of meat attached to a thin bone, and then a platter of desserts: glazed fruit tart, chocolate cheesecake, flamethrower-seared crème brûlée, all the shape and size of a half dollar. "This is simultaneously the best and worst meal I've had in a long time," says Felix.

We watch Precious serve other tables. He holds his whole body as though at arm's length. The way he collects dishes and carries them off, his posture folding napkins in the corner when he thinks no one is looking. I can't place it. Someone with a pinched face walks up to him, and the air surrounding Precious's body snaps in.

"We just started installing this group show," says Felix, gnawing now on the bone that had the sliver of meat on it. "At the gallery. Normally I like installation. Hanging paintings, figuring out the lighting. It's straightforward. But something about the show we're putting up now is making my bosses lose their minds." She takes a long pull of white wine and makes a sommelier face, swishing the glass under her nose. "Musty," she says. "But my two bosses, I don't think you've met them, they're one of these hyper-rich power couples. They have a place here but live mostly in London. In the past ten days they've flown back and forth between there and here at least six times. Coming and going, in and out. One will land in JFK, spend an afternoon in the gallery freaking out about one of the melting sculptures, and then they'll take a limo service back to the airport right as the other lands."

"The sculptures are melting?" I ask.

"We're debuting an artist who only works with animal fat," she says. "Anyway, it's my job to coordinate my bosses' plane tickets. And they're renovating their Manhattan place right now so they need a new hotel room booked every time they come in, but they're insistent that they only need a daily room, one day at a time, and not some weekly arrangement I would only have to book once. They say I shouldn't spend too much money, and that the next time they come in will be the last. But the hotel rooms have to be super nice. They have to fly business class." She wipes her mouth. "I feel like, after an already long day in a room at freezer temperature so the fat sculptures don't melt, when one of these two motherfuckers comes in and starts yelling at me about whatever, as I'm arranging for their spouse to stay at the presidential suite somewhere," she gestures with the bone at Precious's sweaty back, "I probably also look like that."

I can't think of anything from the bookstore that matches the atmospheric pressure I'm seeing pass over Precious's body. He's one of those balloon people in front of car dealerships, arms flailing in the wind. A machine powered by a black hole. When we get up to pay, he stares at us for a couple seconds before seeming to recognize who we are. One eye travels far to the left then snaps back into place.

□ □ □

I wake to the sound of sawing. It sounds like it's coming from everywhere.

In the common room, I find Precious sitting cross-legged on our lopsided couch, looking down at his own face on his phone, recording himself.

He holds up a hand before I can say anything. The sawing sound stops, then starts again. His hand means wait. I look at my feet, then at the ceiling, trying to find the source of the sound, but also trying to not yawn so loudly that it will ruin whatever Precious is doing on his phone. The morning, blue and cold. His hand stays up, arm extended toward me, one finger in the air.

Then I see it: The wall behind Precious's head breaks open, then instantly closes back up. I step toward his now wiggling suspended finger. It happens again. The wall flickers in and out of movement, glitching out. He's poking me in the ribs. I feel like I'm still asleep. We remain still for a few seconds, him staring at his mirror image in the phone, me pressing into his index finger and blinking, unable to get a closer view of the wall, which ripples. It isn't until I follow his gaze that I understand what's going on. On the screen, I see Precious's face, his flailing hair, and behind that the blades of a saw pushing in and out of the frame, jutting through the wall behind him. Sawdust drifts toward the phone. A happy flash of metal in the morning light that is gone and then back again, short bursts of saw blades through our common room wall. There is a long, silent pause—and then the saw bolts a sharp angle through a patch of wall right next to Precious's face, the sight of which makes me jump back and yelp. Precious flinches so hard his phone jumps out of his grip and onto the floor.

"That was perfect," he says, hunching forward to stop the recording.

"Get away from there," I say, "Jesus Christ."

He rolls off the couch and sits cross-legged on the floor, facing the wall. "This construction," he murmurs, scrolling through the video for the exact sequence of stillness, face-proximate sudden saw, yelp, flying phone. "Do you think if I posted a scary enough construction video it could take down our landlord somehow?"

"They're going fucking crazy over there," I say. The wall behind our couch is cut open. We watch this happen.

"I'm going crazy," says Precious. "Every day it's something. Eventually we're going to wake up and the windows will be gone. Something like that."

I finally yawn as loudly as I need. It comes out as a scream.

"They're going to come in and board the windows while we're asleep. That's what they'll do. Look at the wall," he says. "So far the response to my construction videos has been, like, *oh, that's so New York.*" He wiggles his finger again saying this. "I want my videos to get to the level where lawyers will work for us for free because they think it'll give them internet clout. What is fame supposed to be for?"

"They're sawing through our wall," I offer helpfully. "All the way through to the other side of the whole wall. I can see it happening."

"I am literally looking at the same thing right now," he says.

□ □ □

Weeks of this, and then I take a bus with Felix to visit her family in Kentucky.

The bus only goes as far as Cincinnati, which is two hours north of our destination, so we wait for Felix's parents to pick us up from the station curb. The air moves with a different kind of pulse here. The birds make a different sound.

We boarded the first bus at around nine last night, then transferred in a gray and yellow-streaked lot somewhere outside Pittsburgh. On the second bus, Felix befriended a man who looked and sounded almost exactly like Ford. It was as though someone had hollowed Ford out and replaced his insides with those of a different person. The three of us spent the ride from Pittsburgh to Cincinnati talking about intimacy, a word not-Ford introduced to the conversation and pronounced in four diligent syllables. *In-ta-miss-y*, deep through the night and into the morning.

All told the trip took nineteen hours, not including this last stretch with Felix's parents, whom I have never met, and who pull up now. Felix waves at their car. Her posture changes.

At around hour thirteen it became impossible to tell whether the guy who looked like Ford had genuinely radical ideas about desire and attachment or if he was fucking with us. He kept finding excuses to say the word *females*, and then he would narrow his eyes at Felix, then look to me, as though seeking some kind of confirmation. What he really wanted was to drive us to his place, which he said was halfway between Cincinnati and Louisville. "Sure," he said, "why not, people, your parents can meet us there."

"You couldn't have just flown," says Felix's dad, loading her duffel bag into the trunk of his car. Felix's mom still hasn't released her from a big hug. Not-Ford looks over his shoulder at us, shrugging and shuffling down the parking lot.

It's the end of October, but Felix's family has decided to call their reunion Thanksgiving. Louisville, the unfettered mass of it, appears as one continuous grove of drooping trees, red except for Felix's family's farm, where there's a pond covered in green algae that seems to produce its own light. I have a hard time keeping everything straight. Felix's many cousins take photos of us: patting the head of a cow, crouching to examine a palmful of algae, shoveling mulch behind the family house. We pile into the open bed of a pickup truck with the family dogs. Her grandparents send me outside to split wood, but Felix takes the axe when no one is looking and does it herself. Her parents bicker. Everyone bickers, except during a brief period a few minutes after dinner when Felix's one white aunt has us stand up and hold hands, going around in a circle saying what we're thankful for.

"Pie," says Felix's grandpa, eyes closed. "Chocolate."

"All the way down from U-Nork," says Felix.

"Who makes salmon for Thanksgiving?" says an aunt.

I learn that Felix's dad is the baby of the family, and that everyone is allowed or even compelled to treat him like a misbehaving teenager. "Come look at what your dad is doing," says a younger cousin, an actual teenager, beaming at Felix.

We left Girlfriend under Precious's weekend care. He sends photos of her sliding into his shirt, small head poking out of his sleeve, tongue protruding.

Felix's parents introduce me to the family as her *close friend*, though I'm almost certain they understand the deal. We sleep in separate bunk beds, with Felix's parents on the floor, in that same room, in a blowup mattress.

Everyone calls Felix by another name, one I've never heard before and which she doesn't bring up when we walk around just the two of us.

I try to say more or less nothing, smiling and offering to help clean dishes.

At the family farm, what we talk about is the difference in pace, in landscape, here versus there. We've been away from the city for forty hours. We describe a muddy trail through the horse-riven center of the green-orange farm, trying to articulate our mutual adjacency to the things we actually want. Felix's job in the gallery. My job at the bookstore. Our faces pressed against the glass, bordering the thing itself. Making something. "Or take being here now, a day's bus away from our apartments," I say. "Listen to all the bugs."

"It's so easy to be right next to something and never experience it," she says.

Our conversation arrives with real weight, both of us eyeing the other and breathing, but when it's done and we pile back into the family pickup with the dogs and a couple sweating cousins, I'm unable to explain what that weight signifies. The thought of a city careening over itself. And then on the other hand a bunch of cows, wild mushrooms. I brought four books with me and consult exactly none of them for the duration of our stay.

"I'm thankful to see the moon," I say at the Thanksgiving table.

Another of Felix's cousins takes us to the front porch and demands we let her read our tarot. Past, present, future. The tarot deck follows some kind of internet youth culture-type theme, the cards bearing new-sounding names. Felix draws the two of shots (young romance), the four of shots (boredom), and The Executive Office (total upheaval).

"Oh fuck," says the cousin, looking at me.

"Hold on," says Felix, "don't explain yet. Let me just look at the illustrations."

A different cousin gifts us home-baked edibles that will keep us stoned through the whole bus ride home. This will become a minor, gnawing nightmare as Kentucky's soft orange gives way to the inevitable vertical gray. On the porch smelling woodsmoke I draw the two of lips (uncertainty), the ten of phones (work), and The Girlfriend. Felix gasps. "Fuck off," she says. "No way."

□ □ □

While we were gone, Precious bought a prayer candle called Rompe Conjuros—Spell Breaker. "It's not like anything else is helping," he says. "Did you know the email address on our lease doesn't even work? I asked the construction guys if they had a number or a better email or anything, but they said they're subcontracted by a different company than whoever owns the building, with it seems like no one on top to talk to either." Precious looks like he hasn't slept, and he holds the candle at his gut while watching us take off our shoes and drop backpacks on the floor.

On the common room table, there's Girlfriend, coiled in the small acrylic chamber Felix purchased to bring her into the homes of snake-sitters such as Precious. *Her mobile unit,* as Felix calls it. "Did you ask them to at least stop sawing through your wall?" she asks, peering into the coil. "Did they realize they were doing that?"

"This is why I think maybe there's a spell that needs breaking," Precious says. "Those guys said they weren't even here that day."

"Sorry," I say, and duck into the bathroom, having held in a considerable shit since before we boarded the return bus. Now I have to shout into the gap under the door from the toilet. "Do you believe them," I yell. "The construction guys?"

"I brought them chocolate croissants," he calls back. "Those guys are my friends now." From under the bathroom door, it sounds like Precious either can't get his lighter to strike or is flicking it in a heartbeatish metronome just because. "They did say they probably wouldn't be back in here for a while though," he says, "so that's good. No more ceiling holes."

"Oh my god," I hear Felix say from the kitchen, "can I try one of your croissants?"

Why is the consistency of shit after traveling always so weird? Normally I'm quick to release, gone before there's even a smell, but at this moment I'm grunting and holding my breath trying to squeeze out anything at all. And then the shitting sounds I fail to mask behind a thin wall and semi-unclosable door five or six feet away from my two friends. The way time concentrates in the body.

I emerge from the bathroom and read the incantation printed on Precious's candle:

ROMPE CONJUROS

Maldita sea la persona que me ha deseado un mal.
No tengo miedo, por que el espíritu de Dios
camina junto a mí. Ninguna fuerza diabólica
puede tocarme o tocar a los míos. Por que yo
romperé el embrujo hecho contra mí.

□ □ □

On nights she doesn't have to work, Felix will invite me up to her apartment, but if I decide to come over it's important for me to leave her alone. She would never say this, but it's true. I'll find her on the floor of her tiny bedroom, bent over one of her projects in the room's half glow—the cold light of her laptop against Girlfriend's red heat lamp—intent on her painting, or collaging, or the assembly of some cardboard sculpture. On nights like this one of her many roommates lets me in, offers me something to drink, and tells me that the artist is present. I sit on her bed, a foldout couch, and watch her work.

Tonight she's perched on a stool Precious salvaged from the culinary school dumpsters, painting thin bands of ink on a thick wooden board nailed into the broadest wall of the room. She tries to hold a conversation during these sessions, and on some nights one does emerge from the quilted silence between us.

I realize I have used the word *work* to describe both Felix's job at the gallery and her making art. But this is wrong. Felix at work sets the conditions for Felix to actually work. If Felix's job paid more she could do her work in a studio somewhere, instead of in her bedroom—and then the surrounding apparatus of galleries and representatives might click into place. She could sell her work, quit working. The remote flickering possibility.

Tonight she wants me to talk to her while she paints. "It can be anything," she says. For a long time nothing comes to mind, but then I tell her about what happened just before she and I met, which was that my friend from back home died. "He had been on a motorcycle," I say. "The car ahead of him swerved and caught his front wheel. I guess he went diving into the median." Felix doesn't look away from what she's doing, so I continue. "It happened right when I started at the bookstore. I thought I might get fired for taking the time off, catching a bus home and then riding back. Someday you and I should do this, if you want, it's not as long as to Louisville. It's not as nice either. Anyway, the funeral was open casket." I open and close my hand, looking for something in the room to hold. "But his body looked like melted wax. Like a drawing from memory. We stood in line to look, touched the coffin, and went back to our seats." The silence in the room turns one full rotation. I keep talking. "Ellis, my friend. We weren't even friends anymore, not actually. That was all I could think about during the service. He and I grew up together, and then there was a sense of loyalty after that. But his whole orientation toward the world. His parents wanted me to give a speech, during the service. I guess they didn't realize we hadn't talked in years. The old man, he was there too, also I think waiting for me to get up and say something."

Felix considers three different greens she has mixed on the wide aluminum tray she uses as a palette. "The old man," she says.

"My dad's dad. It was mostly family friends, relatives. A lot of speeches about God. Finally someone I didn't recognize got up and delivered a series of stories about Ellis. Stuff I had heard but didn't actually know. Ellis in training. Ellis learning the proper way to kick down doors. Ellis the cadet, the trooper. In one story he's in Baltimore kettling in a bunch of protestors. Behind the plastic shield. *That was his brush with history*, this guy said," I say. "A few years later Ellis stagnating, Ellis going private." Felix changes paintbrushes. "Whatever that means. He starts building cars. He builds a motorcycle from parts. In the next story he's in a three-person biker gang, which basically just means that he and two other cops-for-hire wear the same jacket when they ride around together. Biker gangs follow the same hierarchy as the police, I guess. Ellis the sergeant getting into fights. Then this guy said, *he loved to ride, and he never wore a helmet*, and the speech ended. We drove from the funeral home to the cemetery, and the rest of that day we spent drinking Ellis's Miller Lites and sitting on his porch."

Girlfriend presses her body against the glass. It looks like she's watching the big sheet of paper with Felix. "I'm sorry," I say. "I don't know why I chose that story. I guess we're getting to know each other's families." I can hear one of Felix's roommates boiling water in the kitchen. "Anyway, that's what happened like a week before you and I met."

Felix's paintbrush sounds like a tree in the wind. Out of nowhere, the smell of cinnamon enters the room and lingers. Am I imagining it? No. It's there.

"I've noticed you tell stories that don't really go anywhere," she says finally. "You meander. I don't mean that negatively."

"Where did you think that one was going to go?"

"Maybe your dad's dad gets pissed and yells at everyone on the porch. Maybe you inherited your friend's motorcycle."

An hour or so passes in silence as Felix works. I wake drooling into one of her many pillows. "You were in my dream," I say, before the boundary between the dream and my speaking has had time to fully assert itself. "You were wearing Girlfriend as a scarf and walking around an office. It was your art studio."

She puts her brush down and turns to me. "Sorry I said your stories go nowhere," she says. "What I meant was, I don't fully know what I'm looking for when you tell a story. I'm looking for a through line."

"I don't mean to be tragic," I say, or I think I say, or I'm explaining that stories are like cities, or that they go nowhere even when something happens, or that her painting is starting to resemble the inside of a book, maybe a head, but my mouth doesn't move as I have already fallen back into sleep, drool accreting into a face-sized crater on the foldout couch.

□ □ □

Felix reads online that snakes don't have eyelids; they have a single, invisible scale per eye. These are called *hard eyes*, as opposed to our human ones, which are soft. "Humans," she says, "always blinking and crying." A grown snake blinks once every few months, and only as it sheds. The eyes peel off with the rest of the face and body, revealing new hard eyes underneath.

Hard eyes withstand a snake's sliding face-first through dirt or wood chips, or whatever, into water. We don't see her for days at a time, and then one morning we find Girlfriend's little cartoon head poking out of a pile of substrate, her hard, obtuse stare coming at a long angle, encompassing everything.

□ □ □

It's still warm enough that we can drive up to Connecticut to go clamming. Precious tells us that he used to do this with his family to mark the beginning of summer, but this year it feels important to do now before it gets cold. It's the season of little trips.

"Why is it that leaving feels impossible," says Felix, who agreed to come along and take action shots of us pulling up clams with our feet. "We get out of the city pretty often, you know? We just left. Why is there this feeling that it's impossible to leave?"

It's five in the morning, the sky already a taut, wet blue. We pass a cemetery, a brief grasp of rivers, and a series of small bridges as I watch my two friends' heads and shoulders from the back seat of Precious's car. What I like about riding around is getting to watch.

We're out of the city, which is haunted, and inside the long corridor of trees snaking above it, which is haunted in a different way. My mind wanders. Maybe I fall asleep for a while as Precious and Felix talk about Precious's new plan, which is to become a part-time birthday party clown. "I need to start paying some of this culinary school tuition," he says. "But in order to become a certified clown for this company I have to go to clown school." I find myself in a spiral thinking about bodies as time, as proof of the thing called time, staring out the back window at trees. Since Louisville, probably, this thought has been stuck in me. Time, bodies, cities, time. "So I'm going to clown school to pay off the debt I'm racking up going to a trade school I started at so I could make money after getting a college degree that can't get me a job but came with lots of debt," says Precious. *Trees are a form of time*, I think. My body, as time, expressing all the time that has already accrued in and around it. This accumulation of time projects out into the future, and so my body changes over time. Felix is asking why clowns, why birthday parties. "Not that it doesn't make sense for you," she says. She turns to look back at me, I think assuming I'm asleep. We look at each other. Precious changes lanes. A few days ago, Felix showed up to our apartment with a gift for Precious: a novelty apron with a cleavage-forward torso screen printed onto it. Their friendship is evolving, is what this gift suggests to me. She has also started referring to Precious and my apartment as *the gender loft* for a reason neither of us can remember, though all three of us agree the name feels right. A gendered continuum passes between us, Felix, Precious, and me. I feel this thought float away from the car, joining the thing before about bodies and time. Looking at the trees. "Just an excuse to get out of the house, really," says Precious. "Anyway I bet it'll be good for some videos, clown school." In the months I've spent in the receiving room lifting boxes, my back has accrued hours of labor time, and it holds this time now as discomfort, pain, while I'm at rest. Sometimes I lie on the floor and Felix walks on me, as though pushing pressurized time out, and that takes time too. *Pain as too much time*, I think, this thought also floating away as we pull into the dirt parking lot. "Gender loft," I say, scraping my foot on the gravel and breathing in the salt air. It's the first thing I've said since we got in the car. "Gender loft," Felix agrees.

□ □ □

Before shedding, snakes enter what's called their *blue phase*, or just blue. During this period they burrow, refuse to move, and go blind as their hard eyes cloud over and a mucous film develops between the two layers of skin, the old layer peeling off and the new layer rising to replace it. The skin continental-drifts from itself—then, time passes, and the snake has to wriggle out of its old coil.

Felix invites me to her apartment to watch this happen. Girlfriend sits piled up in a corner of her tank, the same position she's assumed for the past week, tucked under one of Felix's shirts. "I don't actually think she's dead," says Felix, "but I'm worried she may have died." She opens the tank and sprays Girlfriend with a garden mister. The snake jerks awake to drink bubbles of water from off her own tail. "What is this thing," says Felix. "What kind of creature is this." The snake stares up at us again, not blue so much as filmy gray. "She needs to poop," says Felix. "Why doesn't she shed."

When Girlfriend moves, it's with the whole body, all at once. She mashes her head against the glass, squeezing, and then she rises through a small opening of her own, old skin. Skin peels away from her face. "This is like watching something swallow her in reverse," says Felix. Old skin bunches up at her waist, if snakes have waists. She steps out.

□ □ □

I forgot to actually talk about clamming.

The gravel parking lot opens to a small beach. One of those Connecticut-type bodies of water, a cape or a bay or an inlet or a sound, a wet place without waves but a long ambient tide. Saltwater. Precious, clammer since childhood, has a system where he inflates an inner tube, sticks the clam bucket into its aperture, and ties a rope from the bucket's handle to his right arm. Waist high in the still water, he allows the tubed bucket to float toward me before reeling it back to deposit a new cache of clams.

But I'm getting ahead of myself. Here's how it works: To get from the parking lot to the waist-high area of water, we have to trudge through a coastline of cragged-out rocks and shards of shells under sinking mud. And, because clamming can only happen barefoot, by the time we make it waist deep I can see seams of blood rising from our feet, dissipating into the dark water.

Felix, perched on the grass, fully clothed, gripping a thermos of coffee and snapping pictures. Precious hoisting the inner tube above his head, tiptoeing deeper in.

In sum, clamming is a matter of feeling around with your feet. A ridge in the mud, a difference in underfoot density as you step: this indicates clams. Precious with his prehensile feet is able to scrape a clam out of its burrow and transfer it into his palm in one continuous motion. I have to roll my shirtsleeve to the shoulder and grab fistfuls of mud—"like Sméagol grabbing the ring," says Precious, "we should watch that tonight"—hoping anything will appear at the center.

According to Precious, it's important to put the smaller clams back. "You don't eat the babies," he says, "you let them grow for next time." He eyes Felix to see if she's taking action shots. The bucket slowly fills with clams, the inner tube making pliant rubber sounds under its new weight.

"I'm trying to think of how to make this into a video," he says, palming water into the clam bucket, "like how do we build suspense or surprise out of grabbing these weird things from under us? Maybe it's a video of us pulling clams and saying *clam!* over and over again. Quick cuts of these wet scraggly humans screaming the word *clam*. But you'd have to come out here with my phone, Felix, if you want to film." The figure at the shoreline doesn't move. "For those closeups."

"Absolutely," says Felix. She unscrews the thermos. "Why do you have to build suspense about something like grabbing clams?"

My technique improves. Everywhere I turn, everywhere I place my foot, I feel another clam. We call this *clammer's madness*. The bucket becomes so heavy that we have to carry it back to the car crimping either side of its bending plastic lip, our feet sinking into the rocks and shell fragments on the shoreline. By the time we make it home, both of our feet are corrugated with cuts encrusted in dried-up, cement-colored mud.

Now we're in the kitchen brushing sand off clamshells with balls of steel wool. Clams in Precious's oversized strainer, clams under the sink going full blast. Felix is unable to bear the thought of them boiling alive, a stunned gasp and rattling declension before death, and so she goes to lie down on my bed, door closed, pillow over her head. The layer of gritty foam bubbling over our biggest pot's lid, and the thin layer of silt that drifts to its bottom. When she wakes up, she can't bring herself to eat any of Precious's clam pasta, Bloody Marys made with homemade clamato. "I'm glad we went," she says. "I had a good time. I just don't understand"—gesturing to the steaming bowls, sourdough cultivated from scratch and parsley lovingly sprinkled over the corpses of shelled creatures—"all this."

□ □ □

Back to snakes. While I'm in the receiving room, and Felix sits behind the semicircular desk in her gallery downtown, we text each other every snake-related question we can think up. Where does the stomach on a snake start? What is the digestive system like, in general? How do they digest bone? Is bone crushed into some sort of calcium deposit, or what? Is this why Girlfriend's shit is sometimes powdery? Why do snakes sometimes have cat eyes and sometimes not? Can Girlfriend, a corn snake, see better or worse than a python, or a cobra? Or a human? Does her sense of smell augment her sense of sight? How, exactly, does her smelling through her tongue work? And why do snakes have forked tongues? Is it to give them a bigger area of, like, smell reach? How do you check the sex of a snake? Felix automatically started calling Girlfriend *she*—not that her genitals would change this. I cheat and look this one up, learn about a snake's hemipenes, which apparently pop right out, and the fact that a female snake chooses when it wants to get pregnant, storing semen for up to five years after sex, deciding. This phenomenon is called *cryptic female choice*, though Felix and I agree that it's not particularly cryptic. But again, still: why forked tongues, forked penes, two headed snakes? What is it about the doubleness of snakes in general? I clock out, take the train to her apartment, and we look it all up.

□ □ □

We also send each other variations on an ongoing question: What separates an artist from a tourist? How are you supposed to know which one you are? I think Felix finds this question embarrassing, so we don't talk about it in person. But it keeps coming up. If I were to, for example, nail a wood board to my bedroom wall and work on it every night, one of us texts, which would I be? Tourist? Say the materials were low-quality and the work erratic. What about if

I wrote songs heard by no one, recorded on my phone? If it turned out that my sculptures will never actually exist, but my planning them—down to the way their shadows move across a hypothetical floor—fills both my time and entire emotional bank? No one sees, one of us will text the other, but it exists. Doesn't it? If you practice and practice. Is it the tourist or the dilettante who slides from mode to mode without expecting to become particularly good at any one? And what about when reading feels more urgent, more active than writing? Or swap *reading* for going to shows, or just walking around. Looking out. A phrase that comes out of nowhere, two bits of fabric laid next to each other, the colors that appear. And what if the majority of the important members of one's community are dead? What then?

In the receiving room, Dima plays *The Chronic 2001* on loop, working on his freestyle and goading Arthur into singing along as he slices open a box from Penguin Random House and pulls out the invoice. He sings something I can't understand, neck jerking. Then Ford squeezes his enormous face through the doorframe and looks down at us for several seconds. The music volume seems to lower by itself. Dima flicks open his boxcutter. I slowly, instinctively reach for the tape roller, which has a serrated edge that I learned a few weeks ago is sharp enough to scrape through denim. Arthur's posture doesn't change.

"Folks," says Ford, unblinking. Our bodies' arrangement in the room makes a perfect square. "Publishing reps are coming by in an hour," he says after a dense few seconds. "Coffee and bagels. If you're not too busy in here."

This will happen every so often: The publicity team from a New York-based publishing house journeys to the bookstore and gives us a bunch of promotional material for free. The massive publishers, who profit off one celebrity memoir a year, or endless sales of

Harry Potter or whatever, usually don't bother with this courtship. At most they'll send some galleys. The publisher visiting us today is New Directions Publishing Corporation, which releases probably eighty percent of the books I've stolen so far, and holds a glow around itself, in my opinion, even just the name.

This is what I'm talking about, I text Felix. Reading as the crossing-over, as a form of doing all on its own, regardless of external validation. The way layered and multivalent relationships can occur while reading, even and especially with the dead. The actual, back-and-forth exchange that happens while sitting in a room, or the train, silently looking at some bunch of papers for long stretches of time.

And then the flood of writers who themselves receive transmissions from their own invisible lines to the dead. I can't see these lines, but I occasionally tug at them. Most recently I've stolen books by Sebald, Lispector, Bolaño, Natalia Ginzburg, all published by New Directions, all translated into English at around the same time and so made into an ersatz, intuitive generation by me, though none of those authors overlapped while they were alive. The depersonalizing of an author into a book, which talks in its own way. I don't know.

The publicity people come in with bagels and have us sit in a circle while they pass out next year's catalog and black t-shirts with their line drawing colophon of the man and the big dog on it. I realize, reaching out to accept all the stuff, that I'm still holding my tape roller, and when I look back at the receiving room I see Dima still in there. *Still don't give a fuck about books,* I hear him rap over "Still D.R.E.," *still shooting Arthur mean looks.* I realize, also, gifts stacked on my lap and in my seat in the circle, small hole in my jeans beginning to fray, chewing on a cold onion bagel, that I am beaming. It doesn't feel like something I can control.

□ □ □

"Haunted," says Precious. "Cursed."

The TV is on. The elevated train casts sparks outside our window. A brief dash of rain on glass, the low smell of reheated clam chowder and bourbon. I am in pain.

"Which one," says Felix. "Haunted or cursed?"

"It can be both," Precious says. "Maybe one caused the other." He's pausing and unpausing a clip from *The Sopranos*, lining the video up so he can screenshot it when someone makes a ridiculous enough expression. Right now, Tony is smirking in a way that makes him look confused, cross-eyed, lips puckering out. "The ghosts haunting us also put a curse on us," Precious says, screenshotting, "or the curse came first but it's a curse to be haunted."

"I think the curse is on New York as a whole," says Felix, "a curse on the whole Eastern Seaboard." I can just make out the bottom of Felix's foot and some of Precious's long hair from the corner of my peripheral vision. "The Atlantic Ocean is cursed. I don't think the gender loft is special in being cursed."

"That's fine. But when a place is cursed it becomes a prime target for haunting, is what I'm saying. As part of the curse." He queues up a closeup on Paulie Walnuts glowering from under his big eyebrows. "We're just getting the blunt end of the curse, right here in this room. Getting haunted."

I hold a bag of frozen okra to my ribs. Breathing hurts, I want to say, but don't because talking also hurts. Felix pats my shoulder with her foot. "What place isn't cursed, though," she says. "This is my point." I am lying on the old man's rug, eyes to the ceiling. The room peripheral, the light changing. The cube of frozen okra—for clam gumbo, which Precious says he'll make if I agree to stir the roux—starts breaking apart under my body heat.

In the past month or so, as a means of blocking out the physical traces of construction now encircling us, Precious and I have become proactive about decorating our apartment, and so, in my periphery, along with Precious and Felix's limbs I also see the edges of a painting by Felix, some promotional posters from the New Directions reps (Yoko Tawada, Fernando Pessoa) that no one else at the bookstore wanted, and a framed print that Precious found in the trash somewhere of two blonde people in a pink convertible driving next to a steep beach cliff, the words LIFE ON THE EDGE emblazoned on the horizon line. "Name the least cursed place in America," says Felix.

Earlier, the shower head shot off its pipe and slammed into my back, knocking the wind out of me and nearly causing me to slip onto the bathroom's tile floor all tangled up in the shower's flimsy plastic curtain. I tried, after flailing around for a while, to wedge the head piece back into its place, hot water emitting from the bald pipe as though from a hose, but this just made it spray everywhere. Water spraying on the ceiling, water arcing over the shower curtain and soaking the toilet paper. I pushed against the pressure, got the shower head to stick for a minute, and then it shot back out again, this time hitting the wall with a smack loud enough for Precious to knock on the door asking if I was okay.

A bit of tile on the bathroom wall cracked with the force of impact. I wonder if my ribs are cracked, too. "Name one place," Felix says. While this was happening in the shower, the fire alarm went off in the kitchen, though Precious hadn't been cooking anything. He had to take the batteries out of the white puck and hide it in a drawer, me watching him, still wet and with one arm to my purpling side. When I looked out the window, I saw the neighbor's black cat staring at us from its little perch on the stove. The lights flickered. "Haunted," Precious said.

□ □ □

Ford brings a rotation of recently published authors to hold signings and talkbacks at the bookstore. Usually the writers he invites are

Columbia-affiliated academics, or poets who all seem to be from the Midwest; almost never a novelist. I've been to enough of these that Ford has started paying me to show up and help. Here's how it works. Dima and I will smoke on the roof of the building, holding open the window of time between the end of a shift and the start of whatever comes next, or we'll walk to the taqueria on Amsterdam and eat on the curb, and then he'll ride his moped home to what he calls *Deep Brooklyn*, leaving me back at the store with Ford—who wants me, since I'm still around, to go ahead and do some shipping and receiving off the clock—until the reading starts. I pour wine for whoever shows up, chatting as best I can with the poets about weather in the Midwest versus weather here, the professors about whether they can help me understand Deleuze.

Every few weeks I'll take Ford's green minivan to curate the merch table at a bookstore-sponsored reading downtown. Today I sit behind a table in a room quiet with marble busts and chandeliers, rugs that look like velvet and high-latticed windows overlooking the street. Everyone is dressed extremely well—and, even though I know some aren't, everyone's nice clothes make them seem much older than me. Like they've lived actual lives, rather than the formless thing I have slotted into.

A group reading with a moderated talkback. Graduate students, adjunct professors, editors, *n+1*, *Guernica*, *Bomb*, Knopf, Farrar Straus and Giroux, Trident Media Group. Someone holds a copy of *The Argonauts* with a bookmark from our store sticking out.

The reading starts. One of the writers compares the process of composing a novel to hanging laundry to dry. "You can string all of these disparate elements together," she says, "and just watch them hang on the line, as if they were made to be so."

One of the writers says you must always metonymize capital. I think he means to say personify, because then he talks about how you must always kill the billionaire. "Fiction is the place where this can actually happen," he says.

One says that writing a novel is like repairing the hydraulics on a car. Then he says it's more like spinning a bunch of different plates at once. "You can't spend too much time on any one plate. The one that's wobbling needs attention. And then the others."

Now I'm going to do something other writers seem comfortable doing in their novels, which is to cite Wittgenstein. In *Culture and Value*, Wittgenstein says this:

> I might say: if the place I want to get could only be reached by way of a ladder, I would give up trying to get there. For the place I really have to get to is a place I must already be at now.

Listen: I arrive at the place I am now again and again. This is not a place of serenity. I pick the ladder up and put it back down, standing in place, staring at it. Wittgenstein says *really*, says *have to*, says *must*, but he also says *I might say*.

It feels extremely likely that I won't get any further than the perpetual fringe of whatever scene they're supposed to have here in New York. This has to do with my relationship to the ladder, I guess, but it's also about my not being connected enough, or mean enough, or rich enough, or some combination of the three, for this industry in this town. Maybe I am simply too slow. The reading ends. The talkback ends. I stay in my seat. About myself in general, I'm beginning to suspect that I don't *want* strongly enough—or maybe it's a matter of quality and not degree. Maybe there's something unsatisfying about the way I want, the valence or thickness or aftertaste of my particular want as I go about the world eating and shitting, paying rent. I don't seem to be playing along even when I do. I realize, sitting around, watching whatever is supposed to be happening around me happen, that I'm wearing my New Directions shirt. I might say: I don't look like someone with any insider information. I look like a fan, or a wage laborer, both of which I am.

□ □ □

When I come home, I find Precious watching *The Office*. I can hear the theme song from the stairwell, the final piano flourish as I push my key into the lock.

"No," I call from the landing, coming in fast. "Not seriously, Precious, hold on, look at me." I kneel next to him. "What's wrong?"

"It's nothing," he says, "it's just an episode or two."

Michael says something then looks at the camera, excited. Dwight looks excited too but in a confused, grotesque way. Jim's face is blank, but then he turns to the camera and gives his long-suffering look.

"I watched John Krasinski hail a cab once," Precious says. "Did I ever tell you that? He's tall."

Cut to Pam, who is giving the camera bug eyes, lips pursed. You can't just watch *The Office* by yourself in the middle of the day. You can't give up so thoroughly before trying everything else. "I'm worried about you," I say, and I am.

□ □ □

Felix's foldout bed is just wide enough to fit both of us, though there's a metal bar between its two halves that digs into our hips, separating our sleeping bodies into two discrete zones. I dream that Girlfriend burrows a hole through her glass terrarium. It's like her head is a drill: She presses forward and the glass falls out of the way, one clear snake-sized passage eked through the tank. She slithers between our bodies for warmth. She solidifies, becoming the metal bar under the bed—hard, static—and then she turns back into something yielding that I can't help but crush in my sleep. She shuffles right up to my face, staring, with her oblong gaze. Her cartoon head. The red light of the heat lamp stays on all night, working its way behind my eyelids and washing out the dream from the inside. Then Girlfriend starts singing: a trembling hum that comes not so much from her mouth as out of her whole body. The rest of the dream blurs. I wake immersed in sweat and an overwhelming sensation of fear.

□ □ □

I return home to find another memo taped to the door of our unit. In massive Comic Sans, it states that construction workers will be coming by in the next twenty-four to eight-six hours to begin instal-lation of a load-bearing beam in our apartment. None of the other units seem to have received this message. I tear it off the door, throw it on the couch, and am showered, clothed, and on the subway for the bookstore when Precious texts, *what the hell.*

"A beam," he says, pacing back and forth in the common room ten hours later. "A load-bearing beam. Where would that even go?" Felix buzzes the intercom and comes in soaking wet.

"Can I borrow some clothes?" she says, heading into the bath-room. "Also maybe a towel?"

I hadn't realized it was raining, but when I look outside I find a single opaque sheet of falling water. It feels like I'm still asleep— and it's only now that I remember my dream, Girlfriend as drill, the red light pulsing into my eyes and soaking up my brain. "What would happen if it never stopped raining," I say. "What happens to New York?"

"We're getting off track," says Precious. I peel myself off the win-dow and throw sweatpants and a shirt into the bathroom for Felix, who is naked and shivering on the tile. "Twenty-four to eighty-six hours," Precious says. "How many days is that?"

"If it never stopped raining," declares Felix, emerging from the bathroom as though appearing onstage, "the buildings would all rot from the inside and topple onto each other." She looks at me, and then at Precious, who is still pacing.

"And how many days will it take once they start? They'll have to bring the beam in here, and then what?" He addresses the ceiling itself. "Do we have to move our stuff?"

"Every train station would obviously be an underwater cave," says Felix. "But imagine the trash. Every street would be a canal of trash. What are you guys talking about?"

"My question," I say, handing Felix the memo and watching her study it, "is do they mean a vertical or horizontal beam?"

"What," says Precious.

"Does this mean they're going to install a beam into the ceiling, flush with the ceiling, or will there be a beam, you know, going bottom-up?" I point at the floor, and then the ceiling, describing an invisible column. "Vertically," I say.

We look around the room, which is just big enough to hold the three of us. Felix gazes at the ceiling. Is it sagging? The sound of rain.

◻ ◻ ◻

That's not all. The work on the unit next to ours continues deep into the night, and when I wake, workers are tearing off drywall and drilling into brick in the lobby downstairs. It seems less construction than excavation. "Leningrad down there," says Precious, now at a permanent pace around the common room when he's not at school. "Or Stalingrad, which one am I thinking of. Berlin." He's working on a fifteen second video that is just four hundred fifty still images of flecks of paint that have fallen onto the floor of our unit and then another four hundred fifty of his own nostrils from various angles and in different kinds of light, sixty frames per second. Boot prints in the paint dust, inhaling nostrils, finger-sized chunks that crack into a dozen shards at a light touch, inhaling nostrils. "It's not going to get any play," he says, "but it's not for anyone else. The next video will be a compilation of me sneezing."

Today went like this: In the morning I was blocked from leaving the building. The normal construction guys, who I have gotten to know a little—working per diem, no insight on the extent of construction to come, but friendly, apologetic about the frequency with which they enter our unit and start drilling, fans of Precious's croissants—had been replaced by a trio of bureaucrat-type workers hanging sheer plastic tarp everywhere. They were measuring the front doorway when I came down and seemed shocked when I asked if I could please squeeze through. They gesticulated at the ceiling, at the walls, looking at each other in disbelief. "You can't be here," one finally said.

The sunlight came in blue through the tarp, browning the bricks, trapping the smell of pulverized drywall. "Right," I replied, "I'm trying to leave actually."

Customers had already begun forming a line outside the bookstore by the time I arrived, and, because Ford hasn't made me a key-holder yet, when I got there I joined in their grumbling. By the time Dima appeared it was a quarter past nine and the crowd had been brought to a boil. "Almost died on the Brooklyn Bridge," he said, jamming his key into the lock, visibly shaking in his jacket. "City is fucked."

At ten thirty, the seasonal UPS workers wheeled in one hundred and fourteen boxes. "What is all this?" I asked. Penguin Random House, Ingram Publisher Services. Dima cracked open a value-sized bottle of Excedrin, then got on the intra-store phone to ask for Arthur. He changed the playlist to something loud. He cracked his knuckles, grasping for the boxcutter.

"Ramping up," he said. "Christmas."

A hundred boxes means free lunch, that's the rule, according to

Dima, whether Ford knows it or not. At noon he took two twenties from the register and told whoever it was on staff to input the difference as petty cash, and then we walked around the neighborhood deciding between the Korean place, the taqueria, the dosa place, and the halal cart, ultimately settling into a booth with two orders of bibimbap and a ceramic jug of soju between us. I realized, sitting there, gazing at his stick and poke tattoos, his expression varying between confusion and disdain after googling *soju ABV count*, that Dima and I have become work spouses. We are a domestic item, engaged in a reliable, daily partnership for exactly forty hours per week. The only other person who understands. Our shared unspoken back pain, the feeling behind the eyes after too long in a windowless room. A million other things. I didn't even smoke before meeting him. So we go on little dates for special occasions.

We received all one hundred and fourteen boxes, lifting with our backs, and then I decided to walk home. Streetlights, moonlight, lights from buildings. I thought: *I can wear shoes that won't destroy my back after a day of work or I can wear waterproof shoes during the rainy season.* I thought: *look, the reflection of a car's taillight in a puddle.* I thought: *I need better glasses, I need dinner, phone's battery is dead, my back, my backpack, my apartment keys.* I got closer to our building. I thought: *what is that?* I could see what they had done to the apartment lobby from across the street, but I couldn't understand it. I stood there, across the street, gazing at whatever it was, and then I crossed the street.

Now, from the landing, where I currently stand, at this very moment, mouth open, it's blinding. Behind the new sheets of sudden glass, where earlier in the day there had been brick and tarp, hangs a gigantic, utterly radiant crystal chandelier. I want to call it *fluted*, though that's probably not right: more like feathered, composed of hundreds, thousands of dangling glass shards, each one clonking into its neighbors, producing an eerie not-wind-chime sound that echoes into the rest of the hallway. A colossal, suspended, feathered glass creature held in tilting abeyance above the construction's wreckage. In a building with no fucking gas. I think: *it's cubist almost.* I think: *gee.*

I follow a meaningless impulse to reach out and touch the lowermost tier of glass shards, holding brief contact with one sparkling cylinder before it slips off its post and shatters at my feet.

□ □ □

I read books that I don't imagine I will ever talk about with another living person. Some books seem not to exist at all, except that I can hold them. They show up in shipments, are crossed off packing lists and entered into the store's inventory, affixed with a price tag and barcode, and then sit on a shelf until they are picked up again by me. Most I finish on the train and look up online once I get home. Reviews, comments and threads, algorithmically recommended video essays. Other living people seem also to read these books, but never anyone I meet.

Books that stay with me for weeks, like a smell, like something only I can smell. Maybe I evangelize one or two of them to Felix. Maybe we talk about a stanza or weird idea or turn of phrase. But the zone of contact, between me and the book, or me and the book and Felix, or me and *books* as a type of experience, holds its shallow, thin band around my brain.

□ □ □

Felix dozes next to me. I stare at the ceiling listening to rain.

An hour ago she came in smelling like pepper and asked whether Precious or I had seen that the doors to every other unit in the building were open. "They must have been painting today," she said. "Some of the apartments you can just walk right in."

I had been microwaving eggs for dinner, bringing them into a contoured yellow sameness. Over the past few weeks, Precious and I have started watching food hack videos, recipes to try on a budget or without prep time: microwaved scrambled eggs that come out a rubber negative of the bowl you blasted them in, or ramen cooked directly inside an electric tea kettle, complete with vegetables. He takes morbid fascination from these videos, I think, but I'm getting mileage out of actually trying the recipes. I removed the steaming puck of eggs from the microwave and then the three of us walked out of our apartment and through the wide-open door of the unit next to ours.

There, we found the wood flooring gutted, replaced with an off-silver woodgrain laminate. We found the rooms subdivided and re-rendered on a semi-triangular floor plan, two walled-off right angles where the mirror version of my room would be, one slivered window at each end of the dividing wall between them. *These are bedrooms*, I thought, failing to imagine a mattress of any size fitting into the triangular space. We found the bathroom fixed into a gleaming backlit mirror reflecting a condescending patch of re-exposed brick, the sink handles long frictionless bars, the shower head a cube, and the radiators crammed into the corner of every room painted the same matte slate as the frames on all the windows, which rotated open to a maximum of probably twenty degrees. We found a combination washer-dryer in the apartment's only closet, an economy-sized dishwasher under the kitchen sink, and a glittering off-silver slab where I had expected to find a stove—until we found the touchscreen at the slab's base and realized that it was an electric stove, near-invisible concentric rings for burners. I turned the stove on; it worked.

"This whole apartment is the big chandelier downstairs," I said.

"Murdered," said Precious. "Totally killed." I took a bite of my microwaved eggs.

We walked back to our apartment and sat on the floor. "You guys are fucked," said Felix.

When an apartment is murdered, this means it no longer functions as human shelter. The zombie apartment that takes the murdered apartment's place instead functions as a hard shell for digital photos, a two-dimensional space bloating into an uncanny third, hostile to all forms of life. Sustained contact with this slickness results in a slow but inexorable sense of terror, maybe taking the form of an addiction, or animal abuse or something. Any kind of violence out of nowhere. Everyone knows this. *Still*, I thought, sitting there: the next generation of Columbia students will move in, pay four times the rent for half the space and doubled roommates. The neighborhood will reconfigure around these future tenants, as it already has around us, but even faster. The corner delis and laundromats replaced with specialty catfish restaurants named after famous white locals who arrived fifty years after Harlem finally ended. The cycle we ourselves have helped push forward will become more and more dumb to its own force as it accelerates. All the displacement and new development, and on and on. "They'll murder our unit next," I said, lying on the old man's rug and closing my eyes, "if they can get rid of us." But then of course they'll get rid of us. They'll raise our rent. They'll keep destroying and rebuilding the units around ours until we can no longer tolerate it. The floorboards will warp under us, the ceiling will cave in, the papered-over hole will grow until it swallows us all—and now, as I fall asleep listening to rain, I remember the sweating yellow disk of congealed matter with a single bite torn into its side, left either to rot or stay exactly the same on the gleaming surface of the functional electric stove in the apartment next door.

I Have Yet to Develop a Skincare Routine

Nothing happens after we stop paying rent.

Still, money escapes me. All of it seems to go toward food. Precious comes home with elephant garlic, Trappist beer, sushi rice, gouda the color and consistency of silk, off-season mangoes, starter cultures for bread, sesame oil, salmon roe, and a bag of three or four scorpion chilis the color and consistency of dried blood. He's infusing the chilis in vodka and teaching me the right way to roll sushi when his phone rings. "It's the clown company," he says. "Got the job. Part time, birthday parties in Long Island." We celebrate with fermented plum handrolls and a shot each of the scorpion vodka. "Sushi rice just needs to be warm," says Precious, "and with a dash of vinegar on there. That's the whole secret to sushi rice." The moment the vodka hits the back of my throat I start to retch. It remains in my stomach for probably one second total before I understand that I'm going to puke. "Spicy," Precious says. I realize, in the brief span of time it takes for me to dive to the kitchen sink and start vomiting, that I've never actually minded the feeling of throwing up. It's mostly a matter of having to watch food leave your body from the mouth, which is uncanny, and in a state oddly similar to that in which it went in, which is uncanny too. "Probably too hot," he says once I've returned, wiping my mouth, nodding.

So Precious starts clowning. Here's how it works. He spends a week training at his boss's rowhouse in Queens, him and two other new hires, both teenagers. At the rowhouse, they're given their clown uniforms, a surprisingly generic outfit consisting of a yellow suit, blue vest, and trapezoidal plaid tie. They're taught how to apply their face paint in under five minutes. The boss, a veteran clown named Samson who burnt out doing Coney Island, explains that while parents have come to expect the red nose and rainbow wig, kids find over-bedecked clowns scary. What you do is show up wearing the old-school uniform, shake a few hands, and then change for the performance.

That first week at Samson's house, Precious and the other two trainees have to choose their clown specialties. Will they be a face-painting, dancing clown? A scarf-pulling, magician clown? Precious goes for balloon twisting, with a special emphasis on the fast assembly of balloon crowns and swords. That week he comes home with several dozen practice balloons and a special pump, rapidly squeaking long purple and yellow balloons into shapes.

After another week, Samson tells Precious that the rest is learning how to flail around gracefully and that he's ready to get out there. Now every Saturday and most Sundays he'll take the 7 train into Queens and share a joint with Samson and up to six other clowns in Samson's undersized sedan—"a clown car," says Precious, "the stories are true"—as they're dropped off two at a time to various birthday parties across Long Island.

He gets paired with a clown named Calypso, who uses the stage name Green Magic. Precious just uses Precious.

The parties he tells me about are the ones where someone's parent, an apparently equal ratio of moms to dads so far, will hit on him, or there's some extravagant child meltdown, or the rabbit fails to materialize from Calypso's vest pocket. Otherwise the general routine has Precious tying off assorted balloon objects by request, balloon-sword fighting any takers in a flash of clownish bravado—usually with the conceit that he's serving as the birthday kid's valiant but inept bodyguard, unless it's the birthday kid who wants to fight, in which case Precious swaps into the role of a dripping, randomly French interloper—and reciting a death speech full of puns and one-liners once he's gored through the chest. When he returns from the dead, he either constructs an elaborate balloon crown or a bouquet of balloon flowers, presents these to the special one, and honks along as they bring out the birthday cake. Then it's Calypso who's on, Precious working the crowd as she sends playing cards through children's limbs and showers the room with silly string.

"You're certified for birthday parties, but the day may come when you're needed for a bachelor party, grand opening, a wedding, who knows," says Samson on speakerphone as we sit around the common room table, pickling plums. "You'd be surprised how many people end up calling on clowns."

□ □ □

I dream that Girlfriend sheds twice. Felix wants to see the skin, but when I try pulling it out of the tank it's gargantuan, titanic. Inside the tank, which is also now huge, I find another discarded shed, smaller around the base than the other but still yards long. "Where is her skin?" Felix asks. "Where is she?" Is she curled in an alley somewhere, body pressed between buildings? Is she burrowing underground, seeking a subway tunnel she can cram through? But I know she's in my pocket trying to get out. Less snake than knife. I feel her as she tunnels into my guts.

□ □ □

Tonight we're both home, and after watching *The Sopranos* and eating leftover birthday cake from one of his parties, we agree to plug my laptop into Precious's TV and look for apartments on Craigslist. It's time.

CRAZY CHEAP LARGE APT 3 BR ST NICH & W182 is $2,400 a month and close to the A train. "We could convince Felix to move in," Precious says, "or find someone else." The photos suggest tightly partitioned bedrooms, the type of wood floor that does not signal merciless construction (being murdered), and a kitchen. All the bedrooms have windows, I notice. Then: "to qualify," he reads aloud, "you need to demonstrate an income of eighty times monthly rent. How much is that?"

HUDGE 2 BED ROOM!!!! NO FEE ... WOW links to a single photo of a red and white room shot on a fisheye lens to make it look huge. *Over $500 Sq Ft.!*, it says. My back makes a little spasm, flooding my body with relief after it passes.

The listing for "NOW" YOUR HOME! NO FEE GORGEOUS SPACIOUS 2BR-SS-DW-MW-RIVERSDE PARK includes descriptions such as "*NO" FEE*, with "*GORG" Spacious 2 Bedrooms* and an UPSCALE "*Full" Bath.* "This one looks good," says Precious, but when we click through the photos we find a studio with a cloth divider passing halfway through it. The owner of this listing has posted it fourteen times with different names: "HOME" IS WHERE HEART IS! and THERE'S NO PLACE "LIKE IT"! and WHAT'S NOT TO "LOVE" ABOUT YOUR "NEW" "HOME"! etc.

"Everything looks like either a one bedroom or a three bedroom," says Precious, pulling out his phone.

<<LARGE>>/ 2BR APT/ NEAR RIVERSIDE PARK & 1 SUBWAY LINE: this one is close to where we live now, but rent is also $2,400 per month, almost my entire salary once halved. "Should we just stay here?" Precious says, swiping.

He cues up an episode of Guy Fieri's *Diners, Drive-Ins, and Dives* while I reach for a book.

Lately, when I read, I become most fixated on the scenes that develop apart from any given novel's plot. The introduction of a character who walks onstage and does nothing, or the interruption of action by the sheer passage of time. Moments that seem to exist in their own pocketed worlds, or which create the world that the rest of the book frantically populates with stakes and payoff, dopamine blasters and power simulators. Yan Lianke describes the nocturnal sound of wheat stalks scraping against the earth as they grow, fertilized by a farmer's blood. William Gaddis has light passing over a maple tree in a long sentence that is itself decadent, heavy, and dying. Rachel Cusk transcribes the annoying day of a random stranger. Kate Zambreno, among others, walks around looking at cats.

The wall separating Proust's narrator from his grandma, or the act of squeezing a turd over an open fire in David Ohle. César Aira sends an unidentifiable steam engine-type machine across the nineteenth-century pampas, Hiroko Oyamada trails a creature that digs human-sized holes and resembles a weasel or raccoon but with hooves, and Kafka maintains the odradek, a deathless spool-of-thread robot animal, under the stairwell of a family home. None of these constructions do anything other than change the air around them. Or, say, Queequeg and Ishmael spooning, I don't know. One idea I've been entertaining over the past few weeks is to enlist Precious in making video adaptations of these sorts of non-moments. An hour and a half of a farmer unable to sleep over the sound of wheat growing—what does it look like? Or how would you film that light passing over that tree? I look out the window, half-thinking, then go back to staring at Craigslist, forgetting the book in my hand. If you filmed *To the Lighthouse*, what you would see is a bunch of people walking around, painting, cooking, then dying. The hypnosis that comes while peering up at stars from the bottom of a dried out well in Murakami. Hours passing this way, real hours, and that's the film. Or G. H. watching a dead cockroach in Lispector, more real hours passing before she finally reaches over and touches it.

I consider asking Precious if he would do this with me, make some of these films, or if he knows anything similar that already exists. When I look over at him though I find that he's watching a cringe compilation on his phone that is so impossibly awful—seconds-long videos of half-screaming half-dancing men, faces transformed into uncanny digital avatars of themselves—that I say nothing.

In total there are five different devices, five different screens on in this room. Guy Fieri reaches into a molten pot of chili with his bare hands and I continue looking for apartments online.

Listings for $2,000 studios and $6,000 one bedrooms. A listing called $1,150 / 150ft2—NO FEE! PRIVATE STUDIO 5MINS FROM 72ND ST STATION(1,2,3 LINES)! shows a slice of a room with a mini fridge, an electric stove, a sink, and a window. *Private studio WITH SHARED BATHROOMS (Professional cleaned daily)*, it says. Precious and I both know that in order to find an apartment in New York you must first hire a realtor. All this Craigslist is just foreplay. A realtor will charge their fee, access your credit score (this lowers your credit score), ask for fabricated sources of additional income—and in exchange they will take you to the secret listings that never end up online, texting landlords in real time to see if a particular unit still exists and learning immediately about the new ones. This is how we ended up in our apartment, following the vicious momentum of the realtor Jordan, who, in a single day, discovered its vacancy, toured it with us and six other pairs of potential renters, ran background checks on both of us (and presumably everyone else), and had us come into his basement office to sign the lease and receive keys. Precious lugging his enormous backpack as we crisscrossed town on the train. "Of course the gas will be up and running by the first," Jordan had said, "and if not you'll just need to call ConEd." As for the construction, well. I remember liking that we were on the top floor.

The listing titled 4BR FOR THE PRICE OF 2! DW IN THE UNIT—RENO—DEAL shows a dense cluster of appliances—microwave, kitchen sink, black glossy cabinets, half-width fridge and oven, a clear stack of shelves behind glass that must be a wine fridge, and a dishwasher you open with your foot—pieced together in a vague approximation of the New York City skyline. It is almost impressive. Then I realize what I'm looking at. *OPEN HOUSE !! MEET THE NEW HARLEM !! FAST & EASY APPROVAL*, it says. The photos are intensely oversaturated, as though taken on a day with multiple suns. Every wide-angled shot shows new silver laminate floors, which in the photos looks like real aged wood.

"It's the apartment next door," I say. "Check it out. Look how good the floor looks."

Precious raises his eyes for exactly one second before making a brief jerking-off motion and going back to his phone. But the photos make the apartment next door look gigantic, ageless, in direct refutation of history or gravity or death.

◻ ◻ ◻

I keep receiving books about radical self-care, and then I keep coming home. In the shower—its head gone, water issuing like a hose—I think I hear construction workers knock on our front door and come in. I think I hear talking, hammering. It could just be the water pressure on my skull. I hold my head. I rub a special tonic that Felix gave me into my lower back.

The pain in my back has gotten worse. Certain days it hits before I've even booted up the receiving room computers. It shoots from my spine to the space behind my eyes. It digs in, an unmoving quantity of pain. I fantasize pulling my eyes out of their sockets and soaking them in a vat of milk for several hours, leaching out their toxins before fastening them back into my head, renewed, virginal.

I heave open the bathroom window. Outside sounds mix with the shower sounds and the possible sound of people doing construction in our apartment.

All the pain I can't kill with coffee or cigarettes, or the Excedrin Dima keeps between our computers. CBD oil, Tiger Balm. I read the label of the tonic Felix gave me, unable to recognize the names of any of the ingredients. From the bathroom window I can see a corner of the neighbor's kitchen, with the black cat on the stove. It doesn't look at me, but if it did the cat would see the steaming torso of a single naked human framed in brick.

There's no one else in the apartment, just Precious working on a balloon animal tableau at the common room table. Balloon gorillas storm a balloon castle occupied by yellow balloon archers and red balloon banner men. He films the siege. "A little stop-motion video," he says. "For the birthday parties maybe." When I look closer, I realize the gorillas are holding balloon bananas, some of them in the middle of being peeled. Balloon peels litter the battlefield. "Or maybe I'll film something with this video playing in the background." He twists off the hollow end of a balloon cannon. "And layer the videos over each other until you can't tell what's going on. Who knows."

"So no one else is here," I say, pressing my fingers against my eyes. Phantom balloon animals gather behind my eyelids, drifting around in a warm orange glow and flickering green. When I press harder, they vanish.

"Go lie down," he says, but ten minutes later I'm on the downtown train. I imagine an icepick placed at just the right spot on my forehead, right above the brow. I imagine someone reaching an arm back and hammering the icepick exactly once, with absolute force and precision, and the pain billowing away like hot air. *Like a fart trapped in my skull*, I think, rocking with the train. Or the pressure buildup that comes before a volcano.

I am heading nowhere in particular. The shape made by the Manhattan subway is a disfigured circle. If I am not careful, I will begin asking myself the elemental question, which is *why stay in this city?* The city that is a body in pain, that is wasted time. A marathon of *The Office* alone in the middle of the day. A slow dilation of time until the next thing happens, whatever it is, something worse. Getting evicted, remaining in an apartment as they demolish it. Why stay? This question is the third rail. Dear reader: I don't mean to be melodramatic about all this. But nothing happens over this course of time except that the sun sets in the afternoon when I'm still at work, so that I see it only in the walk between subway station and bookstore in the morning, so that my sense of time becomes more stretched and yet somehow less taut than it was before, baggier, so that sleep becomes something that makes less and less sense to me on a purely argumentative level, so that it becomes something I do less often, on a purely practical level, so that my body begins to hate its own motions, its ins and outs, including, I guess, the losing argument of my skull's contents, whatever physical process occurs in the corridor of my body that is also where thinking happens, so that I have a headache every few days that feels like this one, which is a feeling of being ransacked. What to do about this genre of basically meaningless feeling? Even a very strong, meaningless feeling? Is it worth writing?

□ □ □

Here's the situation: Every week I deposit four hundred and ten dollars into my checking account to add to the few hundred to even sometimes a thousand dollars already there. Before we stopped paying rent, nine hundred dollars would need to be set aside per month, plus another seventy or so for utilities, leaving one and one-fourth paycheck, six hundred dollars, for everything else. Another few hundred goes into student loan repayments, three separate bundles accruing interest at a rate of six point eight percent. With rent out of the picture I consider putting a few hundred more per month toward this, student loans, but I also consider luxuries like going to a doctor. Maybe a masseuse. I'm weighing my options. Meanwhile the balance in my checking account reaches unprecedented figures: two thousand, three thousand dollars. I buy a pair of winter boots. The battery in my laptop explodes overnight, inflating like one of Precious's balloon animals to a swollen, distended globule leaking what I assume must be lithium over my IKEA desk. I buy a new one. Monthly metro cards and lunch during the lunch break. My account dwindles again. "Try having a car," says Precious as we sit in the waiting room by the docks after his RAV4 is towed a second time.

□ □ □

I dream that Girlfriend keeps changing. I look at her and she's herself, a yellow corn snake with the orange diamond pattern running down her back. But when I look again, she's a tarantula, the size of my head at minimum and covered with a dense array of thick, clear hair. This new, spider Girlfriend emerges from her tank and crawls up my arm. In the next dream—or the same dream as before but interrupted by a long stretch of nothing—Girlfriend, snake again, lifts herself up and sprouts lizards from her head. The lizards are also her. They scatter from the tank to hide under the fridge in Felix's kitchen. We spend the rest of the dream looking for them, recording videos of the underside of the fridge with the flashlight on, hoping to spot various Girlfriends in the replay, unaware that in the next room she's producing more and more lizards from her head, and that they're scattering everywhere.

When I wake up, I find that I am heaving a fifty-pound box of Penguin returns onto a buckling stack in the receiving room. My shoes are tied, my shirt is the right side out. Dima, on the phone with a distributor's call center, says *thank you so much* numerous times. He holds a packing slip and punches something into the number pad on his keyboard.

The point-of-sale and inventory software is according to Dima the same program the store has been using since the late eighties, and does the old computer interface thing where instead of a vertical line that indicates where you're typing there's an opaque rectangle, so the last character you've typed is always blocked out against the screen's blue. My first week here Dima trained me to tab in and out of screens, use the number pad and keys like Page Up and Page Down to move around. It is a sort of video game, one with its own visual language and a memorized system of input. Codenames and acronyms. It is also a bottomless chute where our labor time goes.

What finally wakes me up from my snake-spider-lizard dream is the long, continuous movement of pain in my lower back. I can feel it take shape between my bones and their sinews.

Theory: when pain returns it is the same pain as before. There's only one sweep of pain throughout a lifetime, maybe ever, though this sweep can be interrupted by stretches of nothing and these stretches can be long. Pain doesn't always begin at zero and build in intensity as the day goes on. Often, these days, if we—me and the pain—left off at four or five, that's roughly where we will pick up the following morning.

Today an immediate six lurches into seven as I meet a fifty-pound box's weight with my palms and bring it to the top of the pile with my lower back. *My body is also this box*, I think. Dense, full of objects, but fraying, secondhand, held together by tape. Ford walks in the room. Dima and I look at each other instead of at him, and then we turn to look at him. I reach for the open bottle of Excedrin and try swallowing a couple pills without water. Ford doesn't break eye contact. The pills make a small dam in my throat. "Hello my name is Dima I'm calling from Book Buffet in New York," he says in one breath as Ford walks out of the room again, "I would like to report some missing stock in today's shipment. Okay. Okay. Thank you so much."

□ □ □

Nobody comes to install the load-bearing beam, and there's no indication that anyone will. We see fewer people inside the building. I slip in and out and encounter no one at all. The construction's refuse, though, the tools, the leftover scraps and trash bags full of plaster and nails, all this continues to pile up. The hallways are crowded with the evidence of work. We hear it happening around us. But we stop seeing it.

□ □ □

I wake to an inscrutable density of clouds and am dressed, underground, and pacing back and forth in the receiving room making minute adjustments to the speakers' volume before I can remove the night's crust from my eyes. It keeps happening. Tossing boxes from the UPS van with my back, tearing off my sweat-dampened pullover and putting it back on, one foot in a thawed-out pothole, shitting the morning's coffee in the windowless employee bathroom downstairs. By the time I clock out the sun's long down. The lights are off in the apartment, and it's completely silent but for the sound of the train trudging around outside.

The cheapest restaurant on the block is either called Burrito King or King Burrito, I can never get it straight in my head which. By the time Precious comes home I'm halfway through a cold plate of nachos, texting Felix, who is just starting her night shift at the gallery.

The d train is down again, she texts.

"I will be a server in a white suit my whole life," says Precious, lighting Rompe Conjuros.

We agree that it is becoming increasingly important to combat winter sadness.

We come up with three plans. Precious's plan is to amass an even greater collection of random art objects. "You can get some pretty good stuff at estate sales," he says, and so the three of us load into his car and drive to a dead person's mansion in Dutchess County. I wonder if Precious has turned me into the type of person who shops at estate sales, or if our mutual impulse to repurpose trash—an inexplicable, strident attraction to doomed objects—is what made us friends in the first place. Felix at least has the excuse of being an artist. At the mansion, we find long rooms full of leather couches, taxidermy deer, cloudy wine glasses, unmarked bottles of pills, handcrafted tables, watercolors by someone's grandchild, and a big vase full of ivy that is, on closer inspection, the hollowed out shell of a missile. "See," Precious says, opening his wallet. "Where else could you find something like this."

My plan is to find every place in the city where we can spend significant time without having to spend money. "No coffee shops or bookstores," I say. "No estate sales." We slip into the Metropolitan Museum through the gift shop. We lie on the floor of the permanent La Monte Young installation in an apartment in Tribeca, pink lights over incense and a loud rolling drone. Every greenhouse and public garden we can find online, though there are fewer than I had imagined. Precious's student ID gets us into a few other places. A patch of perfectly preserved dirt in a white gallery in Greenwich Village. Churches. It's too cold to walk across any of the bridges or take the ferry. "Libraries are free," I say. "Maybe libraries are the last free place."

Felix's plan is to start doing yoga. "There's a studio in Morningside that holds donation classes a couple times a week," she says, "with these panoramic windows that overlook the street." When we get there we find the room already full, decked-out yoga students in devotional poses engaged in long pre-class breathing. The instructor's name is Serge, and he whispers into a microphone attached to his face, though the speakers are behind us, making his presence all-pervasive. "We'll start on the floor," he says, looking right at me but whispering over my shoulder. He comes over to correct my posture several times, pressing down on my knees in a way that shoots clear, undiluted pain through my back. "Easy," he says into his microphone. Somewhere in the shift from downward to upward-facing dog I feel every one of the bones in my spine crack in a rapid ascension and for one second experience pure pleasure. Someone makes a loud, sea lion-type moan during a difficult pose and Felix and Precious are almost instantly trapped in a coil of laughter, trying to keep it down but egging the other on with little snorts, faces going red. Eyes closed during corpse pose, I hear Serge tiptoe through the broad room, coming up to Felix on my right and then to me. Then I feel his hands on my forehead, smelling close to lavender. After class, Serge guards the exit, holding a collections tin in one hand and giving everyone on their way out a final moment of personalized physical contact with the other. We line up behind the person who made the seal noise, the three of us holding a couple dollars for the tin, but as we exit Serge gets it all wrong and the air changes for the rest of the day, re-inscribing the parts that had already happened with a dull thickness: He thumps Felix on the shoulder, calling her *my man*, then softly holds Precious's elbow, calling him *my love*, then looks somehow through me and hesitates before saying *thanks for coming* as I place a five in his little bowl.

□ □ □

"It's Hanukkah," says Precious, to no one in particular.

Felix is embroidering a snake into her shirt while watching one of the Werner Herzog documentaries about ice. An hour ago I made a whole presentation about wanting to spend the day reading—"I only ever read on the train anymore," I said, "and it feels like if I don't reclaim reading as something I do because I enjoy it and not just because train-riding time has to be filled somehow, then I'm losing an important part of myself," I said, "and I will thin out of existence, cease to be"—but since then I have slid comfortably into watching the documentary too, head in Felix's lap.

Outside the rain delays into snow. "What does Herzog care about?" says Felix. "Like what's actually at stake for him when he makes a film, other than just documenting some strange thing? What does he want?"

"It's Hanukkah," Precious says again. "We should make something. We should make jelly donuts." On the screen, someone in Antarctica saws a perfect cube of snow out of the ground and pulls it up.

"I just can't imagine being him," Felix says. "What is he thinking?" Outside, the snow picks up an insistence as leftover rain on the fire escape freezes into a clear patina on black. It's difficult for me to square the weightless, shapeless noise building outside with the cubes now being piled into a small ziggurat in the documentary. Something very loose accreting into a kind of base metal. I probably look like a dog in Felix's lap, moody eyeing whatever's around.

"Come with me to the store," says Precious from the kitchen. "We need jam and some powdered sugar, and probably more vegetable oil. We're making this shit."

"Does vegetable oil freeze?" I ask.

"Everything freezes," he says, throwing Felix and me our coats. For a second I'm in total darkness, Felix's stomach growling against my ear, the smell of rain and denim radiating from her jacket.

By the time we make it outside the snow has coated everything in a layer of silence. Already there are fewer cars out. We watch a tow truck slide downhill, brake at an angle in the middle of the street, and then just stay like that, engine running, lights on. It does this so slowly and quietly it seems almost deliberate.

The silence builds as we walk to Fairway. The numerous grades of height in this part of town, as we walk, become staggering for me to think about: all the different angles at which snow can fall, the minute vectors of speed and momentum determining where any given flake will land, out here, in a part of town that crisscrosses over itself at every point, from the part of Riverside that becomes a big bridge after Grant's Tomb to the overlapped highway to the elevated train to the buildings themselves positioned on different grades of hill—and then every stairway and balcony and alley holding everything together—all the way down to the river, which must have its own topographical variation and depth underwater. *Can snow sink*, I think, but don't ask. Some of it travels into my mouth, melting on the tongue.

Inside Fairway, squeezed between shelves of oil and vinegar, we find Ford. He's with his family. I duck around the corner and turn to study a jar of peanut butter, but he recognizes my slump and pulls in close, peering down from his gigantic head. His family thrashes around in every direction, three shopping carts between them. "Predicting major snow," he says, face the color of a stoplight. Felix walks up; Ford observes her. "Major, major, folks," he says, tossing a grape into his mouth and walking away.

Outside, the snow has become the whole story. Precious bought more food than he had claimed to want—specialty mushrooms, olives from the big barrels, sour cream and potatoes for latkes, salmon, mead—and hoists two full shopping bags over his hips as he trudges through the snow. "We should have brought rope," says Felix, "tie ourselves to each other, like in the Herzog." Precious moves ahead, his walk swift even in all this, fading from view for a few seconds of total white. His long legs.

"In an ice age," he calls back to us, against the wind. "What happens to New York in an ice age?"

In an ice age, the city's buildings fall over, inundated by a snow that doesn't go away. The city's glass folds seamlessly into ice. Probably the bridges' cables snap and the frozen roads crumble. Most important, though, is that the Hudson and East Rivers glaciate themselves out of existence, developing a contiguous shelf, New Jersey on one side, Long Island on the other. In an ice age, Manhattan is no longer an island, therefore, is no longer anything.

It's a nice thought. Back home, Precious hands me a bowl of potatoes and a peeler. Our coats drip in the hallway, pooling little estuaries into the dust and pulverized paint drifting from the hole in the ceiling. Felix says something about homemade eggnog as she rummages through the spice rack. "What movie is that," says Precious, "where it's New York in an ice age?" He's plugging his computer into the TV, tabbing open one of his backdoor streaming websites that comes with a bunch of popups for porn games. YOU WON'T LAST FIVE MINUTES, says the ad before Precious clicks it away. "*Day After Tomorrow*," he says. "Jake Gyllenhaal." A potato peeler is more or less a boxcutter: the same flick and hold, a tender pressure applied to the width of the blade. When I finish with the skins Precious hands me a cheese grater. "Do you remember this one," he says, cracking eggs into a big bowl as the movie begins.

"Darling Precious," Felix calls from the kitchen, "can we do an egg barter? I need a few yolks for this nog." So Precious performs one of his half-culinary-student half-clown bits, separating the eggs from their yolks by passing them back and forth in their own shells, hopping on one foot and then the other.

"This was like the hot-button issue in my middle school," he says, nodding at the TV. "I remember screaming at kids on the handball court about global warming being real. Their argument was that it still snows, so the earth can't be that warm."

"What happened to Herzog," Felix says.

A newscaster in the movie says *I'm here at the Global Warming Conference in New Delhi, where, if you can believe your eyes, it's snowing!*

"Global warming," I say.

Potatoes grate like cheese. Easier, actually. The majority of a potato, like the majority of a person, is water. Jake Gyllenhaal looks scared to die in a plane that crashes through freezing clouds. The heater in my bedroom spurts to life, causing the rag I've jammed into its broken piece to expand, then drip, forming another chalky estuary on the floor. Precious hands me an onion to grate, and so I cry, grating it. Sniveling. Felix hands me a glass of eggnog and returns to her embroidering. The eggnog tastes like semen and nutmeg. I am instantly drunk.

"Hanukkah," says Precious. In our little apartment, the gender loft, not exactly warm but not cold either. The smell of frying potatoes and onions, the threat of jelly donuts later.

But still, also, behind everything: the fraying edges. The something-else that looms over the three of us, though I can barely see it. We play at apocalypse. We continue doing the same stuff.

□ □ □

"Why would I want to read about shit that never happened?" says Dima. He's holding a copy of *Housekeeping* and waving it around. "Make believe people! Stories to give you feelings. You walk away happy, you have a little comfort, you buy some more." He throws *Housekeeping* into a box and brandishes a copy of *10:04*. "Why would I read this either?" he says. "Nothing on purpose! Reheated nothing. Do you have any idea the kind of world we live in? Does it not anger you?"

□ □ □

I grow accustomed to the particular tenor of this particular bookstore. Its dimensional qualities, its size and smell, the way sound carries from one aisle of the sales floor to another. The intra-store phone, the way it carves out a low silence when it rings, and the crackle of the PA system interrupting the piped-in music for a second on either end. The piped-in music, which is always either Ford-mandated cool jazz or some new hire's candy-level pop or else nonexistent. The rapid rotation of new and seasonal hires, who come from Fordham or Hunter College or CUNY or Columbia in accordance with Ford's fetish for cultivating a veneer of intellectual purity throughout his bookstore by hiring extremely educated children of the owning class for its public-facing positions (this according to Dima). The predictable look of shock on an overeducated salesclerk's face as they realize the customer talking to them assumes they're stupid. Most of all, the stock, which passes through my or Dima's fingers every day. Nothing comes in that we don't interact with in some capacity. The two of us applying price tags or removing plastic wrap or stacking books onto one of the red shelving carts and sending them out, or else finding stock quantity discrepancies on an invoice versus what actually arrives. The academic texts special-ordered by Columbia professors for their classes and reading groups, the sudden box full of Edward Said or Hegel that we set aside for some public intellectual the salesclerks all seem to know personally, who will often send a faceless intern to come collect.

On lunch breaks, if it's too cold out, I'll wander the sales floor stacks and observe the new configurations of spines. A book I received a day ago wedged between two from several months prior, a gathering history of material presence I can chart. The affinity books share when they occupy the same shelf, and the wild disjunction of two books with opposing vibes having to coexist. These thoughts rise to the surface as I walk around. The unarticulated sense of ownership I begin to feel over all these books, over books as a whole.

Then Felix and I have breakfast with a friend of hers at a cafe in Brooklyn across the street from a bookstore I've never seen before. We go in and it's an entirely different thing: not just the smell and size, but the actual books lining the walls, and, somehow, the tenor of the books themselves—their shape, the way they take up space, their sense of *being there*, I don't know. We find the same ubiquitous new releases near the windows, but beyond those I find row after row of titles I've never seen before, complete collections by authors I could swear were made up. "What is all this shit," I find myself saying. Authors in distant places and times, yes, but then also authors who seem to belong not just to other literary traditions but other planes of reality. The multiple book dimensions stacked on top of each other, with the smallest cracked-open windows passing light and information through them. Authors who seem not to exist writing the pull quotes on the backs of books by authors who seem to be willing themselves into existence there and then in my hands.

I begin to suspect that almost none of it is real. There are not actually people buying and reading these books—and if I were quick enough I could open one and find it blank, catch the unprepared reflection. "So what," says Felix, "you thought you knew everything?" The nonexistent author, plus that author's nonexistent editors, proofreaders, graphic designers, agents, printers, book reviewers, bloggers, readers. That's not all. The seeming presence of nonexistent writing groups, literary cliques, MFA programs the author may or may not have attended. The conferences and readings. The author's mentors and rivals, their pet peeves and influences, the author's favorite authors and those authors the author refuses to read out of principle. The circle widens and widens. Whatever The Fuck Press, and their print-on-demand titles that all came out in the mid-2000s in the United States and now exist as 90 percent pulp and 10 percent ignored back stock in the corner of some used bookstore in Brooklyn.

Have I only ever listened to The Beatles? Have I gone through life thinking the only color is red?

"At least they can be pulped," I say to Felix out of nowhere, several hours later. She looks at me. "At least they do decompose. I mean, they can be recycled. It's not like a lithium battery or something."

"Absolutely," she says.

□ □ □

Snakes' tongues are forked in order to better track the trajectory of scent left by prey. Felix texts me this in the middle of the night. *They smell in stereo*, she says. *Can you even fucking imagine?* The snake's constant movement, a rope twisting itself into and back out of tension. The straight line of the snake flicking out its tongue and judging by some unseen apparatus left or right, hot or cold. Constricting and releasing. My phone buzzes under my pillow as I dream about it.

When I visit Felix's apartment she lets me hold Girlfriend, but first I have to pluck her out of her glass tank. "She hates this," Felix says, opening the doors. "A huge hand coming in for a grab." Girlfriend, if she wasn't awake before (it is impossible to tell), jerks to life at my touch. She flicks her tongue, gauging my hand's many smells. We hold for several seconds like that, fingers hovering over her coil.

She doesn't snap when I pick her up. She glides over my arm, cradles near the clavicle, and proceeds toward my neck, smelling in stereo, pushing around the skull, wrapping her tail around my glasses and pulling them off my face. She finds a rest spot under the collar of my shirt. "Dark," says Felix, "warm." Her head emerges from under my sleeve. Her tongue flicks.

The rest of the night we spend taking turns reading aloud from a book about snakes that I special ordered and then stole from the store at Felix's request.

Every culture has its snake cosmology. World serpents, snakes containing universes that only come into being after the snake uncoils. The threat of reality collapsing on itself because the snake wants to sleep. The seven-headed snake ferrying Vishnu and Lakshmi over the Ocean of Milk, and then that same snake churning the same ocean into butter. A snake with the face of a human woman creating humanity out of clay due to boredom and the lion-faced snake trapping the infinite soul inside the mortal body for unknown reasons. Gargantuan snakes that carve river tributaries into the earth as they plow through rice fields, seeking the ocean—and tiny snakes slipping through unseen portals into the underworld, ferrying secrets. Then we have the coupling snakes struck with a stick by Tiresias, an indiscretion the goddess Hera punishes by transforming Tiresias into a woman for seven years. "Aha," says Felix. The snake and the shifting underside of gender; the murkiness and uncertainty that is where gender and snakes both happen to live. "Iconic, penis-shaped," says Felix, when we get to this point, "obviously. But look at the ouroboros. Endless vag. Both and." Girlfriend has by this point burrowed under her half-log. She peeks her nose at us through the substrate.

□ □ □

A change in the air. On the train Precious tells us about his most recent birthday party shift, which was held at the restaurant of some famous chef. "He's one of the reasons I moved here," he says, swaying back and forth. "But I wasn't allowed to say hi. They hired me out as a mime and expected me to stay in character as soon as I got out there." On the crowded subway car my mouth more or less falls into Precious's hair. The smell of sweat. "His restaurant has this beautiful courtyard. I think it used to be a convent or something, I remember seeing it on TV. The kitchen is right in the middle of the courtyard, glassed off in a big cube. I wanted to look at his setup but I kept hitting invisible barriers. At one point I mimed preparing a meal, and that got his attention. I specifically mimed his signature thing, which is to grate a ton of pepper onto everything. He might have been a little offended."

We arrive at our station and push out. I find myself locked in a back and forth with a woman trying to board the train as I exit, both of us mirroring the exact movements of the other before finally breaking out of the spell and moving on. The light changes from interior orange to interior yellow.

Felix tells us about the group show at her gallery. "The cubes of fat are melting again," she says. "My bosses are back to flying in from London every few days. I don't know why they think being in the room with these cubes will do anything. One of them comes in, says to do something, and then flies home, right as the other one shows up and says to do the opposite thing. I'm beginning to worry. You can almost smell it from the street."

The night is lower than usual with fog. Not fog. Something dense holds in the air, some thickness, though I can't see it. It packs our bodies closer together as we wind through a thicket of students crowding the entrances of various buildings.

"For me it's the Christmas-Hanukkah rush," I say. "Ford keeps talking about the other shop location where I guess they go nuts over the holidays. The *sister location*. Flooded with decorations and holiday music. I guess the rush gets so intense a line wraps around the block. But our location has almost entirely dried up. No one wants to associate us with Christmas."

We come to a halt at the entrance of a small restaurant. Precious looks up from his phone and scans the block. "I think this is it."

He ushers us up a narrow staircase and past a set of double doors. He slides open a paper divider and pockets his phone, smiling. "This is definitely it." We enter a dark room: polished wood, a rounded-off bar, a low crenelated ceiling, and a carved-out booth overlooking bay windows that we squeeze into, instinctively rubbing the woodgrain as we slide in.

"Warm," says Felix.

"I heard this place is the real deal," Precious says.

Every drink on the menu costs a minimum of twenty dollars, but we're here. Cocktails made with screwpine, barley-almond syrup, mace, egg whites, pickled plum, grilled pineapple. Not all in the same drink. Tea-infused gin, balsamic honey rum, torched maple bourbon. The last ingredient on one drink we fail to order is just *iron*. Do they mean like a chunk of iron? Felix and I miss the comma between *mushroom* and *bitters* on the description of a drink called New Moon and assist Precious in explaining to us how and why mushroom bitters are made, filling in gaps, the three of us happy to be sitting here, talking louder and louder with the rest of the bar as it fills. We talk about the glass chandelier in the lobby below the gender loft, the layer of powdered glass that has been growing beneath it. Every day another little crystal falls off. We talk about the recently installed security cameras in the landing, in the hallway, up the stairs. Nobody seems to have moved in, but the units one floor below ours have been completely murdered at this point. "End of the damn world," says Precious, who then launches into a description of a video he wants to make at culinary school, something complicated that involves installing his phone as a hidden camera inside an oversized croissant. "Croissant POV," he says. I am listening, but in a way that allows all the noise from the rest of the room to fill me up at the same time. The bartenders wear tuxedos. Above the bar there's a long painting of a thin crescent moon surrounded by an almost floral arrangement of skulls. Only one of the skulls corresponds to a human head. Felix tells us about her newest art piece, a paper sculpture that has taken over her bedroom, slowly encroaching on the area around Girlfriend's tank. We have consumed six cocktails total by this point (averaging forty dollars each plus tip), so it's difficult to follow what Felix is saying and impossible to tell whether this issue arises at the level of input or output. Her sculpture sounds like it tracks the material progress of Girlfriend's body as it grows: a snake's random walk. She doesn't use any of these words. The skulls in the painting next to us seem to shimmer. "I came to the realization," she says, spearing a nib of candied chili from her glass with a toothpick, "that what I've constructed so far is only a model. A diorama. The actual piece, if I built it, would be too huge for anyone to install. Too big for New York."

"Like a maze," says Precious.

"Like a building that wraps itself around the others," says Felix. "A city enveloped by my sculpture, filling its gaps. Reverse engineering." It starts to flurry outside. The sky looks so weird. "I don't know if that's what reverse engineering means. You see what I'm getting at. The sky brought down into the city, a city sky, a reverse skyline."

"Concrete," says Precious.

"Glass," I say.

"No," Felix says. "What? No. Paper."

Ten More Notes about Work

1.

Ford moved me to the sister location. One day he walked his whole body into the receiving room and asked me how I'd like a promotion. Arthur and Dima just stood there. "Receiving manager," Ford said, and, "big shoes to fill, folks," and, when I asked if it meant I'd get a raise, "anything is negotiable."

2.

The sister location looks nothing like the flagship. Here there are too many tote bags, finger puppets of dead authors, vegan leather purses and backpacks, seasonal greeting cards, soaps, hand creams, exotic white feather lamps, pillowcases knitted in Peru, winter hats knitted in Nepal, gloves with special webbing at the fingers for texting, tea sets, candles, Swiss Army Knife-esque contraptions, calendars, music boxes, wrapping paper, Christmas ornaments, waterproof flashlights, incense, menorahs, aprons, angular clocks, sailboat figurines, hot air balloon figurines, not-Lego put-it-together toys, recycled paper notebooks, dazzling teen-oriented notebooks, cold European sophistication-type notebooks, quill and ink sets, ethical baby toys, inscrutable poof objects, picture frames, magnets, scarves, cell phone cases, old timey-looking posters of bird skeletons or flower cross-sections or different fishing hooks, reading glasses, chunks of varnished driftwood, salad tongs, and self-help picture books with titles like *Bad Bitches' Guide to Adulting* and *Mindfulness Now!*

The other difference between the sister location and flagship is that here there is no back room for shipping and receiving. What I have instead is a narrow desk adjacent to the registers, right on the sales floor with everyone else. A constant mountain of boxes protrudes into the stacks, where I labor, exposed, dangling, like a tooth. Customers wander behind the boxes and watch me work. A desperate look in their eyes usually means they want to know about the exotic white feather lamps, and how much they cost.

3.

My receiving desk is also where the punch clock lives. As a manager, with a new regular salary of $500 per week before tax, I am no longer required to clock my hours. At the same time, as a manager, it becomes important for me to remind everyone on staff to clock in when they begin a shift and clock out when they leave so they can be fully imbursed at the rate of either $9.50 or $10.25 per hour depending on whether they've worked long enough to be inducted into the union. I didn't know about the union until I was promoted out of it. I remember the raise.

Ford has someone make me a company email address, and now I get a new message every half hour:

> Subject: *MPS return*
> Body: *what are we doing sitting on this? acct near another freeze, hustle up folks*

Subject: *marimekko*
Body: *coming by with a haul .. Mora should make room*
.. wait til you see this stuff

Subject: *xmas pty tonight 8pm pisticci 125 la salle*
Body: *it will be tonight, see above. ho ho ho*

4.

Instead of Dima, I work with Hannah, Mora, and Joyce.

Hannah is having everyone take the official Harry Potter Sorting Hat quiz, followed by the Patronus quiz. The holiday season's frantic rush—when we sold more in a week than in a normal month, and Ford came by to install temporary cash registers on the other side of my overgrown pile of boxes, where he more or less lived, ringing people up and cracking elaborate jokes and taking selfies with certain customers' dogs and performing acts of racist violence on other customers (more on this later)—has ended. The store sits empty. We have time for things like personality tests.

My house comes up Ravenclaw, which leads Mora, who oversees the sales floor's various display tables and showcases, to eye me and say *of course you are* as Hannah comes in for a triumphant high-five. My Patronus is a bat. Mora sorts into Gryffindor, her Patronus a seal. Joyce, who does the Kids Section, is outraged to find herself in Slytherin and storms back downstairs when her Patronus comes up as a weasel. Hannah, along with being in Ravenclaw, has a raven Patronus. She's starting the magic wand quiz when the phone rings. Every time Hannah answers the store phone she recites the full *thank you for calling Book Buffet, this is Hannah speaking, how may I help you?* speech, even when she knows it's Ford calling. Her wand is like two feet long.

5.

Today Hannah has control of the store's music. We listen to the same fifty acoustic guitar songs as every other day she has control. Fifty songs, or three and a half hours of music, stretched over an eight-hour shift. In some of the songs the guitar is swapped out for a mandolin. Some of the songs you can barely hear, more a trembling than music. She never sings along.

Someone hauls a sloping pile of books to the registers on one of the red carts. "Is that the MPS return," says Hannah, shaking her head at all the copies of *My Struggle: Book 5: Some Rain Must Fall* we ordered but never sold. "You know we're late on that?"

To start a return in the sister location, walk downstairs, past the Kids Section, through the back hallway, and past the break room, then slam against the metal door that opens into the long storage-type zone where we keep the trash, the broken-down cardboard boxes organized by size on a wire shelf, the bags full of packing material. At the end of this area there's another door, and if I kept walking I would end up in a narrow alley we share with an upscale-seeming Chinese fusion restaurant. I've tried striking up conversation with the people who work at this place during smoke breaks, but discovered the mutual appreciation, maybe need, for silence.

6.

Subject: *xmas merriment*
Body: *yes you can bring a +1 but let me know now now now*

When I return upstairs with my packing material and broken-down boxes, I find Antoine, our block's UPS driver, leaning over his hand truck and peering at the computer on my desk.

"Money," Antoine says when he notices me.

"Antoine's doing the sorting hat," says Hannah. She puts a hand on his shoulder. "This is a hard one. Would you rather be liked, trusted, imitated, praised, feared, or envied?"

"I'd rather be on a beach," he says, turning from my desk. "How many today?"

I lean the pile of broken-down boxes against the desk, where they remain for one second before slipping into a cardboard puddle on the floor. "Come back in an hour," I say. "Probably twenty."

"I'm going to say *imitated* for you," says Hannah, though Antoine is already carting his empty hand truck out the door. "Only a few more! Which road tempts you most?"

UPS drivers in Manhattan make a base rate of like thirty dollars an hour, with an active workers' union, insurance, and regular paid time off. Antoine reminds me of this when he finds me smoking in the back alley, clutching my back. "You could ride with me," he says, "I could put you on this route. It's all easy shit minus the bookstore. Even the seasonal guys make more than you do."

7.

Five hundred dollars per week is more than $9.50, then $10.25, an hour, but not by much. The open face of the storefront looks right out to the street, interrupted only by a sheer pane of dirty glass. I'm surrounded by merchandise. It is a kind of packing material. I'm surrounded by other people. Hostile customers. Hannah, Ford.

Here, where there is no Dima, no space for secret backroom conversations or the licking together of packing peanuts. Where everything hangs in the open.

I consider how it would feel to become obliterated by alcohol during the lunch break. I consider the pros and cons of tranquilizers, Valium and the others with scary names. I text Precious, who says he can purchase these from his clown boss Samson any time.

The receiving manager before me quit in a fury—Ford only offered me this promotion in order to fill a suddenly vacated role. Have I moved forward in any conceivable way, taking it? What would happen if I reoriented my life around a job such as this? Is it possible— would it be something I would want—to fasten this labor into some meaningful shape?

I build a cardboard box, scan the copies of *My Struggle* into the system, and pack them spines facing out. Memoirs by comedians, thrillers made into already-forgotten movies, memoirs by child stars, cookbooks from a display table about Hanukkah, poetry by famous novelists, nineteenth-century novels with new covers and gilding, last year's guidebooks to Paris, Brooklyn, Montreal, memoirs by reformed cultists, poetry for weddings, famous cats through the ages, how to identify the new mental illness, how to identify authoritarianism. Bubble wrap goes between the books. I tape the flaps shut. Customers mill around my growing pile. After sixteen boxes, the UPS labels print.

"Money," calls Antoine from the street.

"Ready," I say. "Twenty-one."

"You got Slytherin," Hannah hisses as Antoine wheels in. "Slytherin, Slytherin."

"Money, money, money," he says, hauling the boxes onto his hand truck and pushing them out the door.

8.

Here's what happened with Ford. A week ago, when he came to install temporary registers for the holiday rush, Ford made Hannah tell him everything she knew about the newest recurrent shoplifter. He gathered the managers in front of the security footage TV, crammed in a closet in the break room downstairs, and told us to take a *mental photograph* of what we saw, though we'd all seen it before. Hannah to her credit obstructed this ritual for as long as she could, I guess because she knew Ford would do what he wound up doing.

"I'll show you the footage," she said, "but you have to promise."

"Show me the footage," said Ford.

"So," said Hannah, breathing through her teeth.

"Yes," Ford said. "Go on."

"So this woman has been coming in every other week and asking for a copy of *The Secret*. She's figured out that Self-Help is on the other side of the store. And then, when the person on staff goes to get it for her, she loads up on merch and leaves."

"She's pretty good," said Mora. "Precise."

"She's fast as hell," said Joyce.

"Play the tape," said Ford.

"I caught her in the act once," said Mora, "and made it halfway down the street after her. She got in a cab. I don't know what I would have done if I'd caught up."

"I know what I would do," said Joyce.

"There's actually nothing you can do," said Hannah. "Once they're out of the store you're legally fucked. It's important you guys know that."

"Play me the footage, folks, damn it," said Ford, and we watched the same grainy video of a middle-aged woman bundling stuff in her arms and walking away.

The next day, and every day until Christmas, Ford personally trailed every nonwhite person who came into the store as they shopped. There was nothing any of us could do. Christmas, Hanukkah. He made two accusations, going as far as replaying the security footage the second time. Mora says she walked in on him pointing to the TV in the break room closet and screaming *that's you* to a woman anyone on staff would have recognized, someone you could have formerly called a loyal customer. Gesturing around the room as though appealing to a studio audience.

This means he walked this woman downstairs, corralled her into the tiny break room, opened the closet doors as she waited, trapped, and then started the security footage, rewinding it to the right spot on the right day in order to force her to watch a video of some other person. *That's you, folks, that's you.*

9.

Did I quit? Did I slash the tires of Ford's minivan? Did I take money from the registers or the safe downstairs and give it all away? No.

10.

I'm still here. Ford strides into the store, lugging a massive box and emitting his loudest *ho ho ho!*

The box is full of Marimekko not-china bowls they couldn't sell at the flagship, over where Dima still is, with Arthur, who is probably at this moment singing. One of the bowls has cracked in half so I superglue it back together. Later I'll wrap it in butcher paper and bring it home. Powder-blue plastic serrated knives with broken teeth I will throw in my backpack with a stolen copy of the new John Keene book. Sample candles that smell like fir trees, thank you cards missing their envelopes, fraying knit hats named after famous actors: these are all mine. Our apartment begins to resemble a castoff version, or a sample-sale version, of the store.

Still Winter

"What kind of name is Pisticci?" shouts Precious through his wine glass. "This is the third restaurant I've been to this week with a fake-ass Italian name. Pisticci is a made up as fuck name." He slurs his words. Everyone is shouting, slurring—here, the same brick walls as the inside of our apartment lobby, the smell of grape leaves, and the low-ceilinged sound of a couple dozen people yelling over each other to be heard. We're in the back room, Ford in his Santa hat presiding over several pushed-together tables, his arms permanently stretched out and his neck stooped, like a vulture. Food comes in waves. Everyone from the sister location, everyone from the flag-ship store, plus-ones, Ford's flailing extended family, and waiters balancing massive platters of bruschetta and carafes of wine, and, behind a vague curtain, the rest of the restaurant, and beyond that, the city. We're one block away from our apartment. Precious sits across the table from me, refilling everyone's cups and readying his phone in case anything worth filming happens. Felix is also here, gesticulating wildly at Dima, who points to a tattoo on his elbow and then at the empty patch of skin on Felix's elbow. A rictus grin passes back and forth. Wine happens. "Folks," says Ford. Hannah and Hannah's loud husband, Mora and Joyce, Dima and Arthur, the people whose names I can't at this moment recall. The important thing is that Ford foots the bill. *Shots*, yells someone. Precious beckons me over to the bar, standing under Ford's gaze as the two of them ready a line of glasses. Ford studies Precious for what feels like a long time and then looks at me, mouth full of smiling teeth. *It's the season of parties*, I think. Time continues to pass.

Earlier, at the sister location, Ford handed me an envelope full of twenties, and then another dozen or so identical envelopes. Christmas bonuses. "Pass these around," he said. It would have been enough money to run off with, leave the city, but I handed the envelopes out instead.

What keeps me acting on certain random impulses and ignoring others? What organizing principle takes effect?

Ford, Precious, and I clink shot glasses, and now I am knocking back something strong and turning to look at Felix. Her presence makes everyone else more real than they had been even an hour before, but at the same time her being here throws everything else into an unreal light, or reveals the seams holding all this unreality together. Precious too.

"A bookworm," says someone, "in the Big Apple."

What is that sense of floating I'm experiencing now? In a room the size of a storage unit, wrapped in brick. Felix, who carries an emotional atmosphere wherever she happens to go, who listens and thinks, says something to Joyce from work, who if pressed I would probably say doesn't exist.

"Bunch of fucking nerds," says Precious.

"I actually don't know how to read," says someone else.

Let me know if there's anything I can help you with, I think. Thank you for calling, how may I help you? Precious films a flaming cocktail drip blue.

◻ ◻ ◻

I dream I'm eating Girlfriend in a sandwich. I decapitate, segment, debone, and steam her, carefully laying strips of her meat on a slab of baguette. The meat is white, almost clear. When I look back at Girlfriend, still in her tank, she resembles an eel or a leech rather than a snake. Flat and wide, her eyes slats. Precious appears in front of me. He says he ate snake once or twice while traveling. He says they taste like leathery fish. The phrase *leathery fish* churns through the dream. Girlfriend writhes her half-body up the glass and into the sandwich in my hands.

□ □ □

"Why did you make some of the work parts numbered?" says Felix after reading what I have so far. She's building a loom out of stretcher bars from a disassembled painting. I scroll through apartment listings online.

"I'm not sure," I say.

"But not all of them. Funny little work songs." By the time Felix has tied in her warp and starts weaving, Precious—we can hear him singing himself up the stairway—returns from an all-day birthday shift. He mixes himself a highball, then hums his way out of the kitchen and produces, as if from behind his ears, a dozen fliers that rain onto our heads.

"Reptile expo," he says, grabbing a flier before it hits the floor. "I found these on the train." One side of the flier displays a salamander-type creature in close focus, straddling what looks like a gigantic pot leaf. The other side is a map of the town of White Plains. "It's happening right now," Precious says, "until the end of the weekend."

So we pile into his car and head north. We pass the cemetery, the frozen grasp of rivers, and various small bridges as Precious and Felix talk about the relationship between their jobs and a specific feeling of humiliation. "At the gallery it's passed around," says Felix, "that feeling. There's almost a smell to it. One person can become humiliated after a bad interaction, being told off by a really condescending artist or whatever, and then they'll write an email and pass it on, that feeling, that smell, to the next person." The trees that blur past barely look like trees. More like hair. "I've been on the receiving end of this, as you can imagine," says Felix. "I come out of the bathroom and have a five-second conversation with someone and walk away feeling just *humiliated*. By the end of the day everyone has it. What's surprising is that the public doesn't seem to notice. They stand there and absorb it, they linger in the room where it stagnates, passing it around, sometimes for hours, looking at the cubes of meat. I don't get it."

We merge onto a different highway. "It's the opposite for me," says Precious. "When I'm clowning, usually the first thing I do is talk to the dad whose house we're performing in. You know, where is your bathroom, or can I charge my phone. Turns out there's a particular kind of Long Island dad who as a type of guy comes *pre-humiliated*. Right off the bat. They can't even make eye contact. I watched one put on sunglasses and a baseball hat when he noticed me walking up to him. This was inside, in a pretty dark hallway." Precious hits a stretch of bad road and we crunch over icy gravel. "Older kids can be like that too," he says. "Me and Calypso do our bits. We sneeze glitter." A truck almost doesn't let Precious change lanes. He blares his horn, clicks on the windshield wipers. "At the culinary school it's obviously different. The humiliation. You've seen it."

"For me," I say, "it's hard to separate humiliation from its opposite. Whatever that is. Dignity." Precious looks at me through the rear-view mirror. Felix turns around. "We're basically trapped in a constant state of humiliation at the bookstore," I say. "Or I don't know. Everything is designed to make you feel like a child. It's a trap, the sister location, you walk in expecting books and get candy and souvenirs instead. And there we are, managers and staff, these idiots selling candy as though they were books. But being so deep inside the humiliation of the trap seems to produce a sense of self, a sense of pride almost, or dignity, for the other people who work there. Somehow. Maybe for me too. It's all just so stupid." Before I can say more Precious hits a patch of black ice and starts to drift, veering a long frictionless left into the ditch bisecting the highway. All three of us release an involuntary, ascending *oh!*—my fingers dig into the headrests in front of me, Felix's arm shoots onto Precious's shoulder. A strange smile takes his face as we wheel back and forth. It sounds like he's singing. The truck ahead of us, the one that had cut us off, strays to the right, peeling out into a complete about-face and still turning. *Oh*, we shout. We spin. The ditch comes close. We brake to an almost-stop, still floating but heading the direction of the road, facing front, the three of us still producing the sound though it begins finally to dwindle.

Within seconds everything's normal again. Fifteen minutes later we're in the parking lot looking at the REPTILE EXPO banner and rummaging through Precious's glove compartment for a cigarette or a flask, anything.

□ □ □

Inside the expo is a whole other thing. Walking around, we see chameleons bred to emit insane, hypersaturated colors. Snakes bred to look like ghosts. Frogs the size of crickets, and then, beside those, toads of almost unbelievable girth and drip. We see a million reptile people milling through the stands, crust punk-type weirdos with alligator tattoos, inscrutable baby boomers, wizards, plenty of kids with their parents. "This is amazing," says Precious, gravitating toward a novelty sunglasses stand and pulling out his phone. Cubbies full of snakes—individuated plastic drawers, each with a different snake in them. I walk up and the person working the booth pulls one of the drawers open, gesturing for me to look inside. A snake with red eyes, a white face and a blue body.

I think of Girlfriend in her glass chamber on Felix's floor. The snake as genetic testing ground. The physical traits of a snake known to breeders such as these reptile people in advance of the snake's actual birth. A clutch of eggs containing embryonic snakes with desirable and undesirable traits, their gloss and sheen, their eyes and nose. A snake that sells well, a snake that receives tens of thousands of views online. The stage on which a snake—any animal— unknowingly sits. The stage of the market.

We move on. We find vendors hawking switchblades, gun holsters, extravagant multipurpose tools, canes with knives hidden in the hilt. A surprising amount of snakeskin boots and hats. "Are those real?" Felix says. "They can't be." Everyone wears their coats inside, and the buildup of slush from several thousand shoes collects around the convention center's darkening carpet.

The smell of reptile and amphibian shit, and then, over that, the smell of something else. We wander to a hotdog stand at the end of the hall. SNAKE DOGS, says the stand's sign. "Can't be," Felix mutters as Precious takes a selfie in front of the sign. "Right?" Drifting over the wood chips, mud, carpet, and the vague metallic current that floats out from the hundreds of heat lamps perched above their respective creatures, there radiates the persistent steam and smell of hotdog, relish, ketchup, onion, mustard.

◻ ◻ ◻

Why am I always thinking about food? Since transferring to the sister location, thirty blocks south of the flagship, I spend the entirety of my shift's lunch breaks wandering around looking for places I can afford to have lunch. My previous routine—which was bulletproof: halal cart falafel sandwich or three cactus tacos from the stand down the street (either option eight fifty with tip)—has been displaced. I start from scratch. Preparing food in advance and heating it up in the break room microwave is out of the question. Salads, no. It becomes imperative that I carve time out of the day to be alone. So I walk around.

In the store's immediate vicinity, I find two Thai restaurants with lunch specials that start at twelve dollars, an old-fashioned deli whose owners ask me if I'm Italian every time I go in and where I will sometimes buy a rind of cheese and some bread if I'm desperate, a Shake Shack with a line of tourists out front, an upscale not-Subway sandwich place, the upscale fusion restaurant next door, a thousand upscale Parisian-type cafes (for some reason), a Subway, and a lone American Chinese place where you can get steamed broccoli lathered in the same sauce they use for orange chicken plus white rice for six fifty. This last place is a bastion. Unlike everywhere else in the neighborhood, this restaurant, KING FOOD, is consistently packed, bustling, vital. One wall a single pane of glass, one wall bare with two TVs in the corners. I learn that it is frequented almost exclusively by other service workers: cab and rideshare drivers, Antoine and the other UPS guys, freight drivers carting around containers of imported wine to the many cellars belonging to the many other restaurants in the neighborhood, retail clerks, dog walkers, and doormen coming in and out, eyes on their collective lunch. The neighborhood's lords seem unable to even see the place from the street. They just keep walking. This is the secret to KING FOOD's strength. The sauce on the broccoli does make me a little sick after.

Still, the lunch hour becomes something I agonize over. It's not just a matter of where to eat. Now that I am no longer required to clock in and out, time becomes an unintelligible presence. Eight hours working and the unpaid ninth for lunch. Nobody keeps track of my time away from the store. Still, despite this, or because of it, for some reason, I either waste hours walking dozens of blocks during my lunch break or I make perfect beelines from the store to KING FOOD and back, crouched on my stool behind the registers reading the news on my phone fifteen minutes later. "Don't talk to me yet," I say then, "I'm still on lunch."

Most shocking is everyone I see walking around. Or when Ford needs some component for a minor construction project he has started out of nowhere and I'm sent to Basics Plus, all the people I see on dates, one spoon digging into tiramisu on the umbrellaed patio of an expensive Parisian-type cafe. So many people in this city seem not to work at all. Glasses of white wine on a white tablecloth under a heat lamp at two in the afternoon, and the type of person whose life somehow contours around such an ensemble. I feel no trace of emotion as I suppress the full-body urge to swig someone's wine off a patio table and shatter its glass on the sidewalk. Tuesday, Wednesday, Thursday, Friday pass.

□ □ □

The old man calls, wanting to know about my promotion. I always forget how much energy he has. *Where does it come from* is all I can think, holding the phone away from my ear and pushing a bleach-dipped brush into the toilet with my free hand as he talks. "How much was the raise?" he wants to know. "What are the next steps for you? How are you leveraging this? You said your back was hurting? Do you really see yourself working retail much longer? Are they still hiding you away in the back room? *How* much? That's before taxes? What? What?"

Lately, when I read, pages go by that I realize later never registered. Some books it's like the words disappear the moment my gaze passes over them. I can piece together a few sentences, and these sentences take shape in my mind, but nothing settles into any sort of sense. I pick up a book and proceed to turn over the contents of my day, pushing the people I've seen and the words I've heard into and back out of different shapes, replaying, for example, the sensation of pleasure and fear on the icy road on the way to the reptile expo. My eyes move, I turn a page. My pulse slows.

A copy of *Demons* that came into the store damaged: I drift through hundreds of pages of nothing but my own surface thoughts, as though instead of a book I held a small mirror. I sit in my full-sized mattress on a shipping pallet below the general glow of a couple hundred Christmas lights that I strung around the room over the summer. My multiple shadows pass over the wall behind me. I turn a page—thinking, I guess, but not thinking. Some books it's a matter of not noticing. It's a matter of being taken by surprise, even when you haven't been paying attention. Or especially then. I read and reread Nikolai Vsevolodovich saying, *What do I care then about people and how they'll be spitting for a thousand years, right?* In the next room Felix and Precious pickle turnips.

□ □ □

Precious keeps threatening to quit clowning. "Even though I'm a balloon animal prodigy," he says. We step over a sweatered bulldog staring dispassionately at the human swiping at its poop with a bagged hand. We walk to the ramen place on the corner to buy two pitchers of happy hour Sapporo and sit under their heat lamp. It's eleven in the morning on a Sunday, and the sun is out.

"I can't face it anymore," he says. "The first bad sign was Samson's basement." He tells me that because he decided to specialize in balloon tying he never had to venture into the basement, where the rabbits are kept, but that at the end of every shift his partner Calypso would pull a rabbit out of her vest pocket and carry it down to its cage. One day Calypso called in sick, so Samson paired Precious with a breakdancing clown named Freddie and asked Precious to put on the magic show himself. *"It's part of the package the family ordered, Samson said,"* says Precious. *"You'll need silly string, trick cards, an endless scarf, and any one of the six rabbits downstairs."* In the basement, Precious found three squat crates, two rabbits in each one, stacked in total darkness. A stagnant, overpowering rabbit stench in a dungeon. "They keep dying," he says. "Samson just buys new ones and shoves them into those crates to die."

I order our pitchers.

That same day, Precious learned about the daytime versus nighttime playlists. "Me and Calypso never bother doing our own music," he says. "We just bring speakers and let the kids play whatever they want. Usually it's, like, Mario music." For Freddie and the other breakdancing clowns, however, Samson curates two separate playlists. *And so which one today,* Freddie (who uses the stage name Droopy) asked Samson in the clown car that day with Precious. *Daytime, by the sound of it,* Samson said, winking in the rear view mirror. *Don't worry. Big daytime.* When they arrived, the kids at the birthday party—everyone there save a few adults in the periphery—were all white. Freddie queued the Daytime Party Playlist on his phone, and played Taylor Swift, Queen, Elton John, Adele, as he danced in his oversized shoes. *"Maybe next time you'll get to see me put on my nighttime moves,* is what he said to me when we were packing up," says Precious, *"when we have a nighttime audience. He said the music's better, too.* Then he tried to rib me with his elbow but wound up hitting the fucking rabbit in my vest instead."

Last story. Samson asks Precious to wear a Minnie Mouse outfit, the kind with the enormous head and gloves, for an outdoor party. "Not a problem on its own," Precious says, taking long sips of beer, "though I did have to go back into the rabbit dungeon to make sure it fit." Costume jobs are easy work for a clown: you show up in character, wave and strike poses, children intoxicated with delight at your presence, no extra labor needed. "Usually it's just moms and babies at costume parties," says Precious. "At this one, though, there was an out of place preteen, and in the kitchen of this Long Island house where I was cooling off, dripping sweat, with the Minnie Mouse head on my lap, this little baby tween walked up and started hitting on me, in the wildest, most oversexualized way possible. In front of Calypso and all the parents, just laying into me." He wipes his mouth and gazes at the sky. "Like twelve years old, biting her knuckles and shit. It was too much."

We down half a pitcher and review the menu for some kind of breakfast ramen. I realize, thirty minutes after sitting down, that I am one of those people eating out in the middle of the day, drinking beer under a heat lamp, on display for all the world.

"Samson pays us under the table, though," says Precious, "so it's like the money never existed. Which is good. It just gets shoveled into the debt hole."

□ □ □

To receive a shipment, I must first stack the day's boxes by purchase order number. This can be found laser-printed on the top left of every UPS shipping label, itself slapped to the side of each box. Shoulder-height towers of boxes tail away from my desk and into the sales floor, arranged by distributor and therefore by shape and size. For example, Hachette boxes are taller and thinner than boxes from MPS, for some reason. One box out of every stack will contain the shipment's invoice, and locating this invoice marks the first step of receiving any given stack into the store's ancient inventorying system. If the conditions at the distributor's factories are particularly good there will be a red sticker on this one box, announcing its INVOICE ENCLOSED.

Hannah-operated acoustic guitar music plays. An invoice from Penguin Random House spills from its box perforated blue. PO number, quantity shipped, quantity backordered. Then the slow, analog procession of numbers down a blue screen. Key in the quantities. Skip over backordered lines, tab up to initial the NOTES section, hit print, then initial the paper invoice by hand and throw this document to the top of the wire outbox with the others. The sound of a couple hundred labels printing, carving a percussive rhythm against the store's quiet. Then the adhering of price tags onto whatever physical merchandise actually exists in the boxes. Everything must be accounted for, all discrepancies noted by the person doing the adhering—usually whoever was hired most recently, perched on a stool behind the vegan leather purses and so simultaneously handling the Ford-mandated side task of sussing out potential shoplifters with an onslaught of customer service—and then this person must report back to me so I can mark discrepancies in my computer. A staff member named Cameron, for example, hired only a week ago, calls up from the Kids Section to inform me that the triple shipment of Scholastic arrived with a missing pair of *Wimpy Kids*, and so I note this. The Scholastic invoice includes the number for the call line in Georgia or the Dakotas at the top right of the page. I note this too. I will call.

Hours pass. Every book gets its price tag. Every gift-type object. Greeting cards, which come by the thousands, must be individually tagged. At the flagship we called this process *labeling*, but here at the sister location, under Ford's saturated fixation on brand-befitted gentleness, everyone has been conditioned into saying *stickering* instead. There is, always, more stickering to be done.

Ford walks in with an armful of papier-mâché deer heads. "Not for sale," he says, dropping them on the registers as though flaunting a fresh kill. His eyes travel across the walls. "Where's Mora?" he says, already walking away. "I have a van full of deer shit."

"Why deer?" says Hannah, refusing to look up from her spreadsheet. The heads are pink and teal, coated in some kind of carpet-type fuzz.

Ford whips around. "It's spring, folks, so we've got to get all this Christmas stuff out of here. Get to preparing our next look." He touches every item on the spinning rack next to the registers. "Cheerful, folks. Pastoral. I'm thinking Bambi. You see what I'm getting at. Spring's new buds."

"It's like the second week of January," says new-hire Cameron, suddenly upstairs. According to Hannah, Cameron and Ford are somehow related, or they're old family friends. Hannah hasn't yet determined if this is a reason to abuse Cameron beyond typical new-hire hazing or if he can manipulate an otherwise inaccessible line to Ford. For a moment her face settles into an unreadable expression, looking at him. It's exactly three in the afternoon, the blue outside closing into sunset.

"I'm sure Mora will love the deer when she opens tomorrow," Hannah says, her voice drenched in hostility. Ford wanders toward my desk, balancing his gigantic head on his neck and smiling. Now he's unfolding my collapsible hand truck.

"High-powered," he says. "Come help me lug these deer."

□ □ □

Three hours later Precious and I take the 1 train to 157th Street and wander around the cemetery before letting ourselves into various apartments with a lockbox code that is the same for every unit.

Precious has initiated contact with a realtor. Marie. "She seems like a human," he says. "At least from how she texts. Too busy to come with us today, I guess. Very trusting."

The first unit is a one-bedroom. "This isn't right," Precious says, but we wander through it anyway. Bay windows overlooking a gray sliver of grass, a bathroom with a bath, closets. A bar dividing the kitchen from a common room-type space that could, maybe, be big enough to house a second bed. "What do you think?" Precious says. He clicks on the stove; it works. "I guess we would have to figure out who gets the bedroom and who sleeps out here." A brief spray of fireworks goes off in the park outside the window. A car alarm triggers.

"What am I saying?" he says eventually. "Of course not. Right?"

The second unit is in a palatial, prewar-style building with a birdcage elevator and stone stairs polished by generations' worth of shoes, each step indented at the lip. *Like bars of soap*, I think, watching the bottom of my chin move in and out of my legs as we climb to the fifth floor. "I don't even know how much these places cost," says Precious. "I gave Marie our budget and told her we wanted two bedrooms and she gave me this list. I guess we just have to trust her." He opens the door into the unit, where we find a museum replica of an old world tenement house. Grease lines the ceiling of the kitchen—which, the unit seems to be basically one long kitchen, with two offshoot closet-type bedrooms (no windows) leading out from the central area. A fireplace holds court over the burnt floor. Piping swoops in from outside. Sconces line the walls. "Oh," says Precious. "I didn't think they were allowed to still rent them like this." There doesn't seem to be a bathroom. He pulls a joint out of his coat pocket and opens the one window, both of us sidling up to its narrow built-in seat. "Someone really old must have died," he says.

The teal papier-mâché deer head suddenly appears in my head, fully formed and rotating. I feel all the wires reverberating up and down my back. Imagine that candy-colored piece of future waste in this ancient room. Over the dead fireplace, presiding. "Folks," I say, just to try it out.

"Forks," says Precious. "Here's something. I used the bandsaw for the first time today." I take a probably disastrous hit from his joint and blink at him. His big hair. "At school," he says. "We spent the whole day learning how to cut slabs of meat with a bandsaw. Racks and butt." He pantomimes for a couple of seconds, waving around the empty room. "There are people in my class who are pretty bad with knives, and a couple of them had never been in the same room as a bandsaw before, or any of those power tools, so I wound up spending the whole day hovering over them, making sure they didn't chop their hands off. The instructor didn't care," he says, "I guess he assumed we had done it before." I begin to feel extremely cold, and then I remember that I'm sitting next to an open window at night in January. *Oh no*, I think. The feeling my back again. "There's someone in my class," Precious says, coughing a little, "who sliced open her finger while dicing tomatoes, making salsa, like a week ago. But she didn't notice, I guess the cut was so deep it didn't hurt, anyway those tomatoes made it into the final batch of the salsa, and so at the end of the day we sampled everyone's food and I just immediately got a huge mouthful of this person's blood. She's really cool," he says. "Her name is Glossy. You would like her. But I felt like I had to make sure she specifically wouldn't kill herself today, pushing all this meat through a big saw."

There's a third unit on Marie's list, further uptown, but we don't make it out there. Instead we wander downhill until we find a diner. We sit in its cold plastic seats flipping the pages of its enormous menu back and forth. A well-lit room full of cups and utensils. "Man," I say. "I didn't want to be high." A plate of mofongo and an entire fish parqueted in a bright green sauce appears in front of us. Either I ordered or Precious did. "Am I eating the bones?" I say. "Am I choking?"

A series of incomprehensible commercials occurs within a TV angled behind me that I watch through the mirror behind Precious's head.

"There's this book," I say now, though Precious looks too absorbed separating the fish from its bones to listen, "where the narrator goes crazy looking at a diagram of the inside of an ear. He starts thinking about all the cavities in his body, and then without meaning to he reverses the image in his mind, so that his body is the cavity, and everyone walking around becomes like a bubble moving through the filled-in negative space of, you know, reality. Solid matter." I keep adjusting my shirt, the same shirt I've been wearing all day.

"What do you think about that?" I say, but we're already walking the thirty blocks back to the gender loft, pumped full of salt, cowering in our coats against the wind.

□ □ □

There was a period when I would transcribe passages from the books I was reading into a document on my computer. Small moments of vividness or strangeness or meaning; I felt as though I had to keep this kind of thing around me. I had to know that I could cue the moments up and recall.

The act of transcribing became an important part of the process. Typing out every word, every line break, triple-checking to make sure I hadn't altered the specific phrasing, feeling my way through the internal logic of the excerpt I had chosen, holding out an unarticulated hope that something about these passages' access to thought would rub off on me. Their access to language. If I felt my way through enough language—strange language, language at the very edge—then I would myself become capable of producing my own.

Years pass, and my document grows. Will Alexander says *one sucks in doubt from a wave of tumbling blister trees*. Thomas Mann has a dying patriarch come to terms with the disintegration of his self into history, and then, in a different book, Mann calls the way chickens walk around *pedantic*. Ted Berrigan says I *sit at my dust-patterned desk littered with four month dust*. Thoreau says *my head is an organ for burrowing*, and I imagine he means this literally.

Inscrutable tiny moments, or details that make me laugh while reading. Kant can't stand kids, for example; he's really weird about it. In his notebooks Freud is always talking about how he *walked vigorously* through Vienna for like three hours every day. I imagine him cross-eyed, face red, vigorous Freud. I start including page numbers at the end of each quote so I can return to the oysters that had produced the pearls. I almost never do return.

At a certain point I realize I've only been reading one kind of author, so I change course. This happens as clumsily as anything else. Claudia Rankine says *the boy turned to the boys as boys do walking into a fist punching through the blackness as glass shattered light.* Anna Tsing says *freedom is the negotiation of ghosts on a haunted landscape.* Anne Carson describes a road trip through an erupting volcano, and this makes me choke up while reading, I don't know why. Mei-mei Berssenbrugge says *physical perception is the data of my embodiment, whereas for the rose, scarlet itself is matter.* This reminds me of a phrase I read in a book that seems to explain Deleuze, but not in a way I understand: *the flower is the relational conduit for a field-wide tendency to expression*, it says. For a brief period everything is flowers, meaning every physical thing seems to hold a secret in itself—not just the books I read without understanding, but the radiating matter constantly surrounding my single body, already a ghost.

Something shifts. The ritual act of extracting quotes from their books begins to feel like missing the point. At the very least it seems greedy, all this plucking. I consider deleting the document. What I do instead is resolve to leave future shining moments inside their books. I become stuck on them, reading and rereading, but I don't transcribe. Do I underline? No.

Someone in a book asks if there's a name for the sound a guitar makes against your hand when you change frets. I think they call it a whine. A maddening, essential question; who asked it? I would have to go back through everything I've read in the past two years to find out. The information is there, an answer, gleaming and cold, but it's hidden under literal piles of superfluous and flamboyant paper. The pleasure I derive from this knowledge, from being unable to locate a single answer but knowing it exists, is almost impossible to articulate. I will try not doing that either.

◻ ◻ ◻

But maybe this is a mistake, keeping the important phrases locked in their books. Because now when I read I gloss over the particulars. It becomes harder to absorb any given sentence or line. I read and the general idea comes to me. Plot points. Some authors use em-dashes instead of quotation marks to represent dialogue. Some books are padded with blank space and sold in an oversized font to make them look substantial. Others are printed on the thinnest possible paper to trick readers into believing they're actually some other, more manageable length.

I find myself less capacious than I used to be, as a reader. Images from books—or from actual life, for example a painting done by Felix that she later destroys, or the way a mass of clouds fill in a nauseating pink against the frozen blue sky—images like these that would previously have latched onto me, which I would have repeated for myself again and again in quiet moments until they became something closer to reflex than memory, these slip through me now, detected for a moment and then undetected again. Recognizing an encounter with something brilliant but knowing it'll vanish against the horizon. I read, and the sound of the train screaming to a complete stop fills me. This is what I remember later.

◻ ◻ ◻

Eight hours watching Ford pull display tables apart and push them back together again, and then I come home to find another memo in the big Comic Sans taped to the door of our unit. It says *Dear Tenant* and nothing else.

It's Precious's birthday. When I open the door—*Dear Tenant* crushed into a ball and thrown into the kitchen sink—I find Felix on the floor, navigating an array of what look like drum machines, Precious silently queuing up one of his cringe compilations on the TV. *Birthday boy, birthday boy*, Felix sings into a toy microphone. Her voice comes through the array as a mashed-together robot's voice. Theremin synth sounds and crushed drums play.

I rain a backpack of packing peanuts onto Precious as a token of confetti and fall onto the couch. Someone in one of the videos tiptoes up to an ostrich (it towers over him) and then flails away as the ostrich torpedoes its head into this person's neck. *Boy boy boy boy boy*, says the robot out of Felix's mouth.

The plan is to drink Precious's first batch of Hot Cheeto-infused vodka and then walk to the abyssal frat bar down the block for karaoke night. "Be prepared for combat," says Precious, measuring our shots and bobbing along to Felix's song, "we're taking that place over."

"I didn't know you made music," I say to Felix.

"These are my roommate's." She dances with her wrists. "I brought her trumpet too. I have no idea what I'm doing."

"Some culinary people are going to meet us there," says Precious. "A couple clowns."

Clowns, sings the robot, *birthboyday clowns boy boy boy boy*.

The vodka is almost good. Felix shoots hers with a gripped-up face, but Precious takes his time smelling his glass and studying its color before testing a sip. *It's the season of parties*, I think. Now Felix seems to be going for a dubstep-type drop on the drum machine, but keeps going for it and going for it, missing her moment.

Precious paws his way to the kitchen and emerges with a full cheese spread. He refills our shot glasses. He prepares a plate of cured fish. He can't help himself: Our birthday pregame becomes a multi-course meal. Felix says that someone in one of the videos looks exactly like an artist she worked with recently, who kept calling her *young man* as he demanded she conjure up another hundred square feet in the gallery. A sprig of fresh dill catches between my teeth. She turns up the volume on the TV and starts looping together audio from the clip—someone at a hog calling contest getting carried off by a gigantic pig—into a sludgy, near-functional song. "Wait for the drop," she says. Precious angles his phone at me.

"Okay," he says, "what's the dance that goes with this song?"

We walk to the bar and order the cheapest possible beers. We drift toward a circle of chairs near the karaoke station. Felix sings along to the track already playing, which is Selena, and is being sung by an older woman to her pool of friends. I realize I've never heard Felix sing before. I look at her—musical Felix.

Precious grabs the laminated song book and is flipping his way to "All Star" when people I recognize from his restaurant appear by the door. They walk up to Precious as though he were both the punchline and the teller of some unspoken joke. Mess his hair, clap him on the back, the birthday boy. These work relationships. The way companionship emerges as the byproduct of meaningless stress.

Precious hurries introductions through ordering a second round— "this is Glossy," he says to me, "you guys should talk about communism or whatever"—commanding an easy center of the multiple social correspondences overlapping in our corner of the bar. His eyes fixed on the karaoke TV, waiting for his own name to appear.

"Hi," says Glossy. I learn that Glossy moonlights as a service-industry labor organizer. She wants to know if I'm active in the New York City DSA. Her right index finger is bandaged, and I have to fight the urge to tell her how much I enjoyed hearing about her blood salsa.

"How does organizing fit with culinary school?" I say instead.

It's the season of parties. Glossy tells me that it was her birthday recently too, and that she and her identical twin held a diaper-themed party at their apartment in Sunset Park. "We told everyone they had to pass the diaper check to gain entry," she says. "Anyone who tried to come wearing their regular clothes would get a disposable adult diaper from us at the door. It was probably the best party I've ever thrown. Imagine a house full of horny nerds trying to flirt with each other in their stupid diapers." She shows me photos, which trigger my fight-or-flight response and immediately recall Precious's playlists of horrifying videos: the man and the ostrich, old people doing the latest dance. Precious has found someone, here, with this Glossy, is what her party photos tell me.

"Disgusting," I say. "Wow."

"You love it," she says, zooming into a fray of dancing adult babies. She tells me about the studio apartment she shares with her twin, Charlotte, and how it's so small they share a bed. "People think we sleep together because we're obsessed with each other," she says, "and we are, but really we are just poor as fuck." She says the word *fuck* like she has to punch it out of her body. In the bar's clatter, her voice emerges as a kind of physical force, the sound of compressed air punched through the emotional system. I imagine Precious subsumed by this person, one bubble eating a smaller bubble.

Someone has queued up the main song from *Cats* on the karaoke and begins to sing. I eye Precious, who eyes a cluster of musical theater-type people, unmistakably Columbia students, who cheer the singer on with self-conscious whoops and wide smiling claps. His desire for combat self-justifies. When I look back at him, I can see that he sees that I understand.

"What can you tell me about his general deal?" Glossy asks, nodding at Precious. "We only started hanging out recently."

Precious and I were assigned to be roommates in college, along with three other people, in a dorm room converted from a one-bedroom apartment in a defunct housing project. "Where Precious and I went to school," I say, trying not to slur my words, and noting with some alarm how early in the night it still is, "the standard for housing was pretty low. Our dorm had mushrooms growing through the radiators. Black mold everywhere. I contracted scabies that year. Anyway," I say, "Precious was pretty famous. He would throw these huge parties just to use them as the backdrop for videos he'd shoot throughout the night. One party was usually good for a week of videos, a couple thousand views in a couple days." When I look over at Precious, he and Felix are arm wrestling. "He studied moral philosophy. In school. It was always good and bad with him, right and wrong. He didn't go by Precious yet."

"He's an incredible chef," says Glossy.

When I look up again, there he is on the small stage at the end of the bar. Precious knows that one person in a room singing "All Star" by Smash Mouth results in the entire room singing along. I have seen him hijack other people's concerts with this stunt. It's all in the maneuvering. And then, once a room has sung "All Star" together, it becomes easier for that room to fall together as a cohesive unit. The cultural climate of a place as generally hostile to survival as this particular frat bar can be slapped into an expression resembling the giving and receiving of real care by a clown singing a shitty song onstage. It's his gift.

It's a tough room though. The table of *Cats* people closes in on itself, and only a few of the chefs pick up on the minor shift moving through the bar. Glossy is the first to get it. She sings along, as do I, as does Felix. The song is as stupid as it has always been. The spell works but only almost.

When he returns from the stage, instead of embarrassment, Precious radiates a scalding pride, which takes the form of an angry smile.

"I'm going full fucker mode," he says.

Someone from the *Cats* table mounts the stage and sings something from a different musical. I don't recognize the song, but it seems ubiquitously known to the room. "Christ," says Felix, who looks as drunk and nauseous as I feel, "do these people think you're supposed to be *good* at karaoke?" Precious lines up a tray of shots, and links arms with Glossy as they take theirs together. Felix and I exchange an identical look. Someone walks into the bar, and for a glacial second this person appears to be Ford. When I look back at Felix she is reaching for the karaoke book. When I look up again not-Ford is gone.

This is how it goes: My body catches up with me and for a while I am crushed by an urgent need to be either asleep or dead, the space between shoulder blades ringing a muffled chime, but then I share a cigarette with a culinary school student whose name I immediately forget on the cold brick outside the bar, and this person has me repay him by pretending to flirt for a couple minutes, and then Precious's clown colleague Calypso shows up and flirts for real with Felix, who responds with a manic, almost anguished energy, and I find that I am no longer so sleepy.

Felix's response to this kind of attention is something I have seen before. She works herself into a froth. When we met, I would get a spill of texts from her in the middle of the night asking laser-targeted questions about my thoughts on longing and memory, for example, or the particulars of my imagined death, followed by a second volley of texts apologizing. She greens under Calypso's pressure.

Meanwhile, the combined effects of alcohol, nicotine, and exhaustion seem to take control of my body. The room whirs around. The person who gave me the cigarette holds a lingering hand on my shoulder. Felix and I again lock eyes, and for a moment I experience total clarity, the third eye rips open, though it is a clarity that if I were to turn around and look at the person touching my shoulder, his face will have been replaced by Ford's. I can feel his breath on my neck.

The *Cats* song cedes to a three-person rendition of the song about America from *West Side Story*. The singers appear to have coordinated a dance routine to go with the song. Cigarette person disappears.

"Fuck this," says Felix now, the America song having ended and her name appearing on the screen. She stomps up to the stage and grabs the microphone. "Good evening everyone this song is called 'Kiss From a Rose' by Seal and the point of it is to be goofy rather than provide a virtuosic performance you miserable little dicks so listen up."

The circle of theater kids grows louder. I watch them convulse in the face of Felix's wild singing. A pit of real sadness opens in me: this city, full of wounded people so jacked up on the promise of making money, or having sex, or whatever it is, that they spread a joyless sleaze over the city's every surface. And us too. Felix up there.

I am waiting for the drop. It keeps almost coming.

Several songs later Felix and Precious are up there together, heaving their way through "Smooth" by Santana and Rob Thomas. An excessively hostile choice—even Calypso and Glossy, huddling across from me, seem to wither. Precious, still onstage, pulls his phone from his back pocket and films Felix singing. The theater people look like they're going to start throwing chairs through windows. Precious films them. He points his phone at me, but I'm too full of beer and fish and cheese and red vodka to do anything.

"Shitposting through life," I think I hear Glossy say.

Calypso makes a show of looking at the time. "Early morning tomorrow," she says.

"And it's just like the ocean," Felix chugs, "under the moon."

Somehow, they've fallen a measure behind the backing track, missing its changes as they honk along to the chorus and spray air guitar over our section of the bar. The theater kids, as though on cue, start singing in time with the song—*or else forget about it!*—as a corrective, but one directed more at Felix and Precious's existence than their fumbling through the song. Someone is actively booing.

Glossy says something about how we're torturing the people who work here. Calypso leaves, which makes Felix—sitting across from me again as Glossy climbs now onto the stage—produce a loud sigh and grab my hand across the table. "Some people," she says, "I can't stand to be near them. They're just too beautiful."

I wonder if the cocktail of malaise and nausea coursing now through my intestinal tract has substituted itself for simple jealousy: not for Felix's attention toward Calypso, but rather for Felix's whole mode of being. Going through the world, talking to everyone, active. I wonder if at some point in my childhood I accidentally knocked out of place my general emotional bank, such that when I should feel jealous I get sad instead, when I should experience rage it's boredom, when I should weep it's a headache then asleep. When, exactly, did the wires cross? Or is this innate to me as a person? A self-obsessed baby fussing through karaoke night. I didn't even get Precious a birthday present.

I say something to Felix. What do I even say? I don't know.

"What is your problem?" she says back.

"Get your shit together," says Precious, though he is grinning, making a gesture as though taking a photo of me with his fingers.

"But actually," Felix says. She covers her eyes with both hands and rolls her head back. I see the red below her eyelids. "Be nice."

The culinary students trickle shapelessly out, except Glossy, who is singing "Livin' la Vida Loca."

In fact we too are outside, shuffling across our street's iced-over brick. Now we're traveling through the pulverized glass portal of our front stoop, past the construction site of our lobby, up the stairs, and once again into the gender loft, sweating as we pull at our coats: Felix, Precious, me, and Glossy.

"We should have brought this," says Precious, starting up Felix's drum machine apparatus and pressing all of its buttons at once.

Birthday clowns, says the robot. *Boy boy boy hostile clowns*.

"This apartment," Glossy says. Precious clicks open the briefcase next to the drum machine and pulls a gold trumpet out of its red velvet negative. He manages to squeeze a single toot from it, then falls next to me on our small couch.

"It's just like the ocean," he says.

I want to reflect here on an underlying, almost vibrating sensation that has dominated every day of the past several weeks, but I can barely keep my eyes open. The repetition of it. The flitting here and there and then coming back home. Days that end in nights. Work and then something else and then sleep and work again. Having fun. How it all seems to happen within a mile radius of our apartment, even when we're far downtown or in some other borough. We take trips.

The room spins—Felix and Glossy exchange a look, and then one of them walks off. The sound of the kitchen faucet.

I want to consider here how everyone I know seems to crave celebration, though nobody seems to agree what for. Or how, if it's not celebrating, then all this activity means—what? A series of more or less constant distractions—from what? The sensation that seeps into the cracks of every thing we happen to do. The assurance that anywhere we go, however we act, there's an unfathomable sameness underwriting it.

Not underwriting. The comforting routine in the tap water that Felix more or less forces down my throat as I cough and burble. The having already done all this as Precious pulls a big sweater over my head and onto my body and lies me down, alone, on the small couch, my feet over its arms.

I guess I am shivering pretty hard. And Glossy being here for this is new enough, novel enough. But then again.

The various minor crises that end in nothing. The burst of some approximation of chaos, filling back again into the regular grooves of our days.

Even Precious's videos turning to one shapeless mass. I can imagine, at this very moment, as everyone crowds around me telling me to just breathe, the long scroll through his many videos. I imagine getting to the end of the scroll and finding gray. Nothing there. Even Felix's sculptures, which never leave her apartment. Even a book: reading it, writing it.

A blade cleaving through the air. My hometown. A blade passing too slowly through flesh. My life here. I can't just go back.

"Okay," says Felix, "alright." And so, what are we doing here, then? At this late stage? Building a family? Or spreading a random, invisible substance—like the theater people's miserable sludge, I think, retching, or like language as a whole—around a more or less nameless city? More or less endlessly?

A series of common and proper nouns. It's possible I see nothing at all.

I want to ask the room some question, but when I open my mouth I discharge a sudden body of fish-smelling puke all over the couch, the big sweater, the wall with saw holes passing through it, my two good friends, and Glossy, whom I just met tonight. It comes rushing and rushing out of me. Fish-smelling, that's right. It does smell like fish.

■ ■ ■

The next morning, I wake early, alert, a perpetual motion machine built on chugging water and peeing clear, steaming ribbons of piss back out. I can't explain it. My head doesn't hurt, my guts equalize, my back feels fine. My body renegotiates its terms.

In the kitchen, there's Glossy, watching as the light through the window moves from morning green to morning yellow. I didn't realize she stayed over. "Breakfast shift," she says, accepting a mug of coffee. Her voice sounds like it's been in a fight.

We pantomime a few stretches as she describes the Korean-Mexican restaurant on Essex where she works, serving up endless pork belly chilaquiles to tourists. "I only started a month ago," she says, "but I think they're already looking for a reason to fire me."

"Sorry I puked on you," I say, but she just clonks our coffee cups together and asks if she can borrow a towel for a shower. Fifteen minutes later, the light in the kitchen a clear blue, she has already left.

When I return to my bedroom I see Felix's sleeping body, a pillow over her head, the sun blaring through the window. I return to the living room. I sit on the couch. I try not to regard the couch's red stain.

Precious spills out of his room, clutching his head. "No," he says, sitting down. "No," he says, as Felix emerges appears a few minute later, filling the cave interior of our apartment with sunlight. He closes his eyes. His phone buzzes. "No, no," he says. Then he looks at it, and says, "okay fine."

Felix doesn't say much.

"Marie wants to meet," Precious says. "We've got listings."

◻ ◻ ◻

The realtor's office is right off the 168th Street station, in a glassed-up complex behind a Chipotle. Marie, younger than I had imagined, outwardly assesses Precious and me as some kind of couple within the first minute of our walking in. Here's how this happens: She shakes both of our hands, smiles at Precious, then looks at me, then turns back to Precious—reviewing, I think, her initial appraisal of his face, his body—and shoots him a different smile than before, and then she turns back to me with a face communicating some new confidence, some secret knowledge. For the rest of the day she will address everything she has to say to him. "It's a tough market for two-bedrooms specifically," she says, walking us out of her glass office and onto the train, "but I've got a few today that look stunning."

The first unit is in a massive apartment complex straddling a wide street that is actually the top part of a long tunnel. Cars pass through a series of empty cubes below us and come out the other side, facing the sun. Their general presence, the cars, fills the air with sound, following us into the lobby but closing out once we're in its elevator. Precious makes a face I can't parse. When Marie opens the door to the unit, six stories up, the car sound resumes. Precious mouths something too long to understand and beelines to the bathroom, leaving me and Marie to wander through the empty apartment. Its configuration is this: a narrow kitchen that leads into a bedroom that itself railroads into another narrow bedroom. A cul-de-sac-type apartment. The bathroom tucked against the entryway. "I'm not sure," I say, opening and closing the door dividing the two bedrooms. "Not a ton of privacy." The toilet flushes. The thought of having to determine in advance when to pass through the other's room. The thought of Precious tiptoeing over my sporadic laundry, maybe with Glossy, at some weird hour when I'm asleep and dreaming about my boxcutter. The toilet flushes again. Marie drifts to the far corner of the kitchen, looking at her phone. I pull mine out and text Precious *okay?*

Shitting, he responds. The highway outside folds into sunlight. *Might puke a bit too.*

The toilet flushes. "The next listing has a prominent living room," says Marie, loud enough so that Precious can hear, "and the bedrooms are at opposite ends." She holds up her phone, which has an image of a hand-drawn floor plan on it. I can hear Precious retch through the wall. Nothing registers on Marie's face. Maybe a slight grimace.

A few minutes later we're on the train again, continuing north. Precious closes his eyes. "You feel fine," he says.

I feel fine. I'm not thinking about it. The living room of the second unit is covered in a layer of clear plastic tarp. It's like visiting a roped-off room in a museum. From our perch at the end of the hallway, we can see into the bedrooms, which look normal, and the kitchen, which has a new-seeming sink but no fridge or oven, just a few dangling pipes. We can walk no further. "The landlord says they're almost finished renovating," says Marie, holding up her phone. "Should be beautiful once they're done." I notice the sound of hammering coming from elsewhere in the building. The familiar noises. Blue tape, gallons of house paint, various temporary objects in the corners of every room. Still, sunlight pours through the plastic.

"Do you think," says Precious, looking around, "that the." He tenses. "The bathroom." Marie makes a noncommittal gesture and slinks into the hallway, leaving Precious to pad over the tarp into a room where I can see a toilet but no shower. The door, caught on a trundle of plastic, doesn't entirely close. "This is so much worse than a regular hangover," he calls through the crack in the doorway. "I feel like there's a second person living inside me," he says, "and that person is shitting and puking everywhere too."

It's quiet for a few seconds. I can almost hear the birds outside. Then: "the fucking toilet doesn't flush."

We move on. "Last listing," says Marie, back on the train, heading still further north. "This one was completely redone a couple years ago." She's reading off her phone. "New kitchen, updated appliances, that's already solid." She looks up at Precious. "Roomy, too, going off the floor plan."

We enter an apartment on the ground floor of a long building slotted into a concrete hill. There's nothing wrong with it, not really, but when we walk in Precious and I both release the same exasperated sigh. The barred-up windows face a wrap-around cement wall. Sunlight drops in brief angles onto the wood floor. I wander around. When I look at the floor again, the patch of light is already gone. "Probably like five minutes of daylight a day," Precious says under his breath when Marie steps away. We dutifully check the bedrooms, which are nice, bigger than the ones we have now. The fixtures and everything else look new. Precious closes his eyes and breathes loudly through his nose, then lurches into the bathroom. I look at my phone, where there are seventeen emails from Ford. The sound of Precious puking and farting at the same time. When he comes back out, wiping his mouth, he says the shower looks good. We cast long shadows over the apartment, three looming, Plato's cave-type figures groping around. Then we reemerge into the beautiful blue day, winter sun a diamond over all the brick cubes.

■ ■ ■

I dream that Girlfriend has gotten loose and is hiding somewhere in my bed. There's an opening in the mattress, and when I shine my phone in there I can just make out her orange coil between the springs. I reach my hand into the mattress to pull her out, but what I grab is a long, thin rat. Now it's like the clown's trick of the endless scarf coming out of the shirt: I keep pulling, and another rat comes out, then another. They're linked together, a chain of salami, rat after rat after rat frantically being pulled out of my bed.

Look How Badly
It Wants to Live

Spring goes like this: I get off the train and buy two bananas from the fruit cart down the street, eat one while power walking toward the store, keys emerging in a dash of sound from my coat pocket, and the other during my smoke break in the narrow back alley. When I get home I find that Precious has bought a new green-yellow bunch, though three or four bananas still sit browning from the last time he went to the store, and so every ten days he bakes banana bread with walnuts or coconut flakes in the little toaster oven Felix bought him for his birthday. But in the flurry to leave the apartment I forget to saw off a piece of Precious's bread or pluck one of the new bananas idling on the kitchen counter so instead I pull two quarters from my coat pocket and give these to the man working the cart. If I don't eat a banana before the store's nine a.m. opening then I am fucked for the day. It ends before it starts. My head pushes through my skull and I thrash around looking for something to hold.

This is my routine, and here is the body I slot through it. Tight spring days, a coiled shape not unlike the baby rats we order in bulk for Girlfriend to eat. I wonder, opening the glass doors of the bookstore to begin another week, about my own capacity for freedom. Deviance from routine once one has been set. I wonder what will happen next.

I scald my insides with coffee at ten and shit in a rushed burst at ten thirty. Such conditions create the demand for either trance or obsession. Small things expand. It's a phenomenon I have been tracking.

Today Ford has control of my attention. "Here's the thing," he says, stacking a pile of books on the floor, "if you don't move, you're dead. Like a shark. I think you're ready to hear this. I'm telling you because you're ready. If you stop moving, you're already dead. Take the sister location as an example. The thing about this location is that it's the breadwinner. Did you know that? The flagship is printed on the tote bags, it's our face as a company, but the sister location bankrolls all that. Right here. This location, next to the park, right up the street from a major museum, you've seen the tourists who come in here, they walk in imagining they're in the market for a book, maybe a notebook with a nice gold lock on it for the niece back home, but what do they end up buying instead? You already know what they end up buying. They buy a bag, a candle set, some moisturizer, a bar of chocolate. Throw in a dozen greeting cards, a whole set, and remember to visit the Kids Section downstairs for those notebooks, who knows what else you'll find? Now pause for a second. Give me a hand with the new display pieces, they're in my van. Come on, come on. That's how it works. Book sales, that's one thing. Books can be a surprising market. Once a year, twice a year, a movie comes out and everyone scrambles to buy the book it was based on. You never know what will sell. I tell Hannah every chance I get, folks, the moment a book has sold, you have to reorder it. I don't care what it is. You never know what it's going to be, you can never keep track of the bloggers or whoever it is these days making the waves, suddenly you can't get enough copies of the block-buster book. But that's one thing. That's all the way down here, do you understand?" He holds a hand at his knees. "So. I'll grab the wheels, these two pieces should come first. Not those pieces, the longer ones. Keep up, folks, I can't stay double parked forever. Now think about the shark. When you're a shark you move in time with the forces around you. You tune your reflexes. You react. I'm trying to train you, right now, to think like I do. When it snows, the shark hangs string lights in the window and plays 'Baby It's Cold Outside.' When it starts to rain, watch me, the shark will come in here with a day's worth of umbrellas for you folks to sell. The clear thirty dollar ones and the twenty-five dollar Toulouse-Lautrec ones, you'll see. Drop those pieces there, then one more trip to the van. Do you understand? The flagship store is like a public service. A brick and mortar, a mom and pop. In that neighborhood in this day and age, just keeping that store open is a public service. On a good year it breaks even. Cold out here. But the shark doesn't stay alive by servicing the public. It perfects its reflexes instead, it capitalizes on every small movement its prey makes, conserves its energy as it moves. I'm talking about the company right now. Yes. We cut a few corners. That's nothing. To stay independent, you cut a few corners. A line is defined as the shortest distance from one point to the other. We take the straight line. Sometimes that means we call up someone like Milton. Remind me when we're done with this, there are some leftover Milton boxes in the back seat, see those, you can receive those later, then give one copy out of every ten to Hannah, tell her to go ahead and shelve them, and you return the rest. Sometimes you take the shortest distance, and someone like Milton helps move you along. I'm telling you because you need to know. It could be you, you could be me. First grab that. Not that, come on, hurry. Warm in here. Is it just you and Hannah today? You drill those pieces together, it should be a full stand-up display once we're done. I've got the toolbox in the trunk, come back out with me, come on, last trip. Grab that box there with the Milton stuff. That one there. Heavy? At least the snow is gone, for now, watch your step, and this reminds me, someone needs to keep better track of salting the storefront, folks, look at this, you could've slipped, we can't have customers slipping and falling in front of our store, we need to start taking care of the area around us, start thinking about the image we project out to the street, I see trash bags out front, if I'm a customer I'm going to keep walking, I'd walk all the way to Barnes and Noble, Hannah, hey Hannah? Hannah, folks, someone needs to salt the area right outside the store, can you put someone on that?"

"It's not snowing," says Hannah. She's carrying an armload of the books we left piled on the floor, and doesn't look up.

"It's not snowing now," says Ford, "but when it does. Here's the thing," he says, turning back to me. His head seems to grow. "I took out a second mortgage for this shop. The sister location. Because I know it's the breadwinner. I know that, maybe not right away, but in a few good years, which is just several good months in a row, breaking even won't even be in our vocabulary. We can turn this whole ship around. Keep the shark moving. It's a matter of the minimum distance between two points. The sister location bankrolls the flagship, the flagship brings a consumer base into the sister location, the public service of the flagship and the brass tacks of its sister. There's no use getting sentimental about it. Books sell however much in a year. We get our forty percent off wholesale, but we have to give members of the loyalty program a ten percent discount on all purchases, plus free shipping, then they come back with their returns, and then there's the stock that doesn't sell the way it should, the event books that should sell fifty copies in one night but everyone shows up with copies they bought on Amazon, God help us, and so, at the end of the day, books bring in however much they bring in. My mortgages. Luckily we're unsentimental about it, folks, and we remember it's a public service, the books. You can come in and read the whole damn book and walk back out again.

That piece goes there. Not there, there. And so you look around the landscape. You keep pace with the forces around you. What do you do? You can never be Amazon, God knows, you can't be Barnes and Noble, but you also can't just lie on your back and die. What do we sell? I'm getting to the point here. We sell books, new stock and used books at the flagship, periodicals, loyalty programs, public readings, kids' books, and, you already guessed it, didn't you, we sell the lifestyle items you see in this very store. Napkin sets, candle sets. Adult toys. But also, more importantly, an adult sense of self. Now this is what sells. This is exactly what keeps us afloat, and in a way it too is a public service, because, listen, because in the back of the mind of every single person who walks through our door there is one lingering and invisible question. Want to know the question? Here it is. *What am I?* Even the tourist, if they walked through our door, if they sought us out, this is the question they need answered. *What am I?* Do you know what you are? Well, luckily for the public, if they walk through our doors, the store answers. A service." He looks momentarily like he's going to slap me. "You've got the drill set on reverse. Give me that. Look. The store answers. The store tells you exactly what you are. But the thing is, folks, the real secret is that the sister location and the flagship offer two different answers to the question. The flagship says, with the full assurance of almost twenty years in business, listen, if you came here, if you walked through those doors, don't worry, *you are a smart person.* A reader. That's what you are. You're someone with an intellectual purpose, a spiritual destination, and the way there is through books. A straight line. That's what the flagship says. The secret though, the real secret, the thing keeping us in business, is that the sister location, this very shop, we say that too, sure, *you're smart*, but we don't leave it there. We dare to ask the second question, which is this. *What is a smart person?* Really think about it. What is a smart person? Someone who reads, fine, but when you put the book down, when you walk out of the store, how do you hold onto that feeling of being a smart person? Think about it. Well, what kind of napkins does a smart, reading person use? What does a smart person's dinner party look like? How should the candles smell? What kind of notebook, pen sets, bookmarks, tote bags does a smart person need, in their everyday lives? And how does a smart person raise their kids? How do you make sure your kids end up being smart, reading people? We answer all of these questions. Most importantly, we provide the shortest distance between the two points, between asking the question and answering it. Again a straight line. You walk in and the question becomes almost overwhelming. Lucky you, though, because your neighborhood independent bookstore provides a highly curated, accessible, family friendly, mom and pop selection of lifestyle products that down to the last one ask and immediately answer those terrifying questions, *who am I* and *what is a smart person*. A public service. It really is. We shouldn't even have to pay rent for a service like that, should we? Why should we? This store is a religious site, if you look at it from the right angle, a not-for-profit, an all-around generator of value."

I wonder what I will have for lunch. I wonder what Felix is doing. Are sharks and snakes related? Are there saltwater snakes?

"One more thing," Ford says. "Let's not forget, in addition to providing a public service, that I employ you kids, folks, you college graduates who come to the city without any skills, needing someplace to start out, a launching-off point, you need help getting off your asses and so I create jobs for the express purpose of doing just that, I employ artists, young intellectuals, I've seen my people go from retail clerk to manager to PhD in the span of a few years, I've seen you start families, I've seen you fall in love and get married, right here in this store, folks. I think we're almost done. But the problem is I've seen my people lose sight of the straight line. The store stagnates. It does, I'm seeing it right now, stagnating, that's why I have to come down here and shake things up. I walk in here and see new hires, I don't even know their names, that's fine, but *they* don't know who *I* am, they treat me like a customer, and let me tell you, if that's how they treat customers, if I'm a customer I'm going to walk right out the door and straight to Barnes and Noble. Because what's the difference at that point? Why employ young quick-witted people if we're going to be indistinguishable from Barnes and Noble on the front of customer service, public service? I'm telling you so that you'll learn. What we need to do is keep the straight line in the back of our minds. We need to keep our reactions heightened. A straighter, more reactionary workforce. That's right. We're almost done here. One last thing, one other thing I'll tell you, and Hannah can confirm this, you haven't been with us for very long, but the thing is, I reward good thinking. I do. And believe me, I can tell when good thinking is being done." He stops talking in order to gaze down at me, a silhouette against the store's fluorescent lights, and then he looks around the store.

When I step back to survey what we've built, I see an enormous spinning display rack, which Ford loads up with *Hamilton*-branded adult coloring books. "This looks good. Come on," he says. "Like I said, a straight line. Labor and reward. I've got some wine in the trunk. Come on, come on. I think we earned it."

□ □ □

Someone bangs on the door of our apartment, but when Precious answers no one is there.

□ □ □

An hour later it happens again.

□ □ □

Otherwise, spring goes like this: Felix and I visit as many museums as we can while waiting for something elemental to change, for the ice to thaw out, for one of us to quit our jobs, for Precious to cook something so spicy we burst into flames. There's a texture now to our relationship that wasn't there before. An ivy covering. She becomes busier with work. One night we have a long conversation about Precious's birthday, my turning sour and exploding, but the conversation veers off track and becomes about Felix's sense of the future instead. A sense of foreboding coupled with nervous energy. Pounding against the glass until it finally shatters. Total doom, except she will be fine. Maybe this was the conversation she intended for us to have.

Everyone's relationships seem to change with the season. Glossy drifts from Precious for a while, unavailable for drinks and unresponsive to texts, but then one day she comes to the apartment unannounced and stays for two weeks. She and Precious solidify, meaning Glossy enters the continuum of our mutual friendship full-time. The three of us now the four of us.

With Glossy there is a quantity of impatience riding the edge of most interactions. She leans forward, nodding into the last word of a sentence, a laugh waiting to emerge from the depth of her throat. It's a quality that clicks into place only after I meet her twin, Charlotte, outside a hair salon in Sunset Park. Charlotte says something, takes a long drag of her cigarette, and then puts a hand on Glossy's shoulder, holding eye contact for an indestructible second before she says the next thing. Glossy bursting at the seams to finish Charlotte's thoughts early, to laugh on her twin's behalf. Her smile that emerges all the time, independent of exterior influence. The rage smile, the confusion smile.

She comes by the apartment with a pound of cheese from the restaurant where she works and we spend the night frying pupusas, flash-pickling cabbage, doing our nails.

She calls Precious *the diva* as he cooks and Felix *you angel* when she gathers everyone's dishes. She calls me *little brother*. Someone says something Glossy finds exciting and she says *get out of town*.

Someone says something painful or obvious and her eyes roll up into her skull as she pulls a dance move, ass way out, arms locked into claws above her chest.

Anyone she doesn't know is *this bitch*. "I will literally poison these bitches," she says with a widening smile as we brush past a gaggle of staring cops.

□ □ □

The sun emerges from behind a blockade of clouds and tapers off a few hours later.

Felix's job takes her to London, and then she's back with a bottle of scotch for Precious and a napkin drawing for me of two penises tangled around each other like snakes made by someone her gallery represents. "This guy was completely smashed when I commissioned that," she says, watching me run a thumbtack through the top of the napkin in the narrow zone above my bed. "But the signature's right there. It'll be worth at least a grand in a couple years."

One day we are lying on the floor of the La Monte Young installation downtown when Felix says *there's something in my mouth*. The room passes from magenta to some thicker, slower color. A tube of incense pulses through the steady drone. I barely hear her. "Like a piece of sand," she says. "I can't spit it out. For a while it felt like I had chipped a tooth and the piece that broke off was rolling around in my mouth. A rock in my shoe, but nothing falls out when I turn the shoe over."

Her teeth look blue against the room's pink. "A phantom tooth," I say.

We lie on the floor in silence. The carpet, the loud atonal rumble. I wonder what the world outside will look like once we leave. "Do you know what I mean?" Felix says, rolling over to face me.

The whites of her eyes also emit a blue light. "Something really small but really coarse."

It was the middle of the day when we came in, but now time seems almost diffuse. A substance. When you lie on your back on a carpet in a strange room for long enough these kinds of things happen.

"This isn't something that is actually in your mouth," I say.

"It's something that won't go away," she says. "I can't stop running it over and over. If I'm a machine then there's a cog out of place. But just one, a small one. Or if I'm a wheel then the finest grit has gotten into the wheels." She rolls onto her stomach. Her long back. "Imagine a breeze in the desert. There are flecks of sand in the wind. Right? And the wind is blowing against a bunch of rocks. I'm the rocks. That's me. Do you see what I mean?"

"Erosion," I say.

"Entropy," she says. "The uncanny valley."

We get up, crack each other's backs, and walk down an ordinary flight of stairs to exit the building. Outside it's the middle of the day. I can still see the room's magenta when I blink. I feel its drone, but only in passing. The regular stimulus of the street brings us back to its terms.

□ □ □

Back home we find Precious preparing borscht. His hands purpled with beet, apron blood-spattered. "Soup's on," he says.

Felix sits on the common room floor and beckons me over. She opens her backpack and pulls out a jar of ink, some surgical tape, a bottle of rubbing alcohol, black gloves, various first aid-type packets, and three long needles, laying each tool in a semicircle around her. "These came yesterday," she says. Then, calling toward the kitchen: "You still want to be guinea pig number one?" Precious makes a kind of yodeling sound in response, then comes over and hands her a bowl full of borscht. They study the needles, Felix sitting and

Precious towering over her. "I've never tattooed anyone before," she says. "But I figure this would be a way to make money that has at least something to do with making art. Apparently the best way is to practice on bananas."

"You're doing it on me," Precious says as he walks into the kitchen and returns with a second glowing magenta bowl. "I'm in a rut," he says. "It's impulsive decisions time."

The borscht tastes like earth, like sharp sweet mud. "What rut?" I ask, though I already know.

"A normal rut." He sits on the couch with his bowl. "Like I'm waiting for the world to end. I had that stomach flu and lost clowning hours, then I got depressed sitting in my room waiting for the bug to pass. Watched all of *Planet Earth*. I haven't made a video since karaoke night. It feels like we'll never move. When it gets warm out I want to start a garden on the roof, but it also feels like it'll never get warm. In conclusion a rut rut, a rut-sized rut." I pull a long black hair from my bowl, describing a momentary pink trail in the air between our faces. "And my hair is falling out," Precious says.

I can feel the thought form in my head and move down my spine before I am able to articulate it. "You're in a rut," this is me speaking, turning to face Precious, and then Felix, "and you've got grit in the wheels. Or sand in your mouth. For me it's like this. Imagine all the grit *taken out* of the wheel. Imagine a landscape with no ruts at all, nothing even approaching a rut. A frictionless place. All the sand has been sieved out of the wind. And then imagine going on like that, never accelerating but never grinding down either." I have never thought about it this way, and as I speak I can't tell if I believe what I'm saying. But something is there. "Which is worse? Too much friction or none at all?"

"I am not particularly fond of this line of questioning," says Felix.

"It's like nearsightedness. Every day I have the feeling that something will change, that I will change, but then the day starts and

I'm off doing whatever it is I need to be doing, and then another day starts. Or it feels like I'm constantly recovering from the last thing that happened, and during the recovery process I forget what that thing even was. And then I start over." Now that I've begun, I can't stop talking. "I mean, I observe. I make observations, walking around. I write what I'm observing. But none of those observations go anywhere. Right? Even if I manage to diagnose whatever the problem actually is, this myopia, this frictionless space, it's just going to stay there, observed by me but unchanged. So what am I for? Reacting to the things around me, but in such a minor, toneless way it is as though I have remained completely still. If you're in a rut you are at least trying to get out of it. Acting on the rut, acting on yourself. If there's sand in the wind then a process of change has already begun, even if it's a destructive process. In my case there is no actor. Just me, a total creation of my circumstances. Part of the landscape basically. Not a shark. Not a snake. A clam." Dear reader: Am I saying all this? Is it possible that I say it, but not in these words?

"Rut is what you call it when deer go into heat," says Felix, consulting her phone, head down. "Maybe Girlfriend will go into rut eventually."

"I was watching a lion chase a gazelle on *Planet Earth*," Precious says. "And all I could think was, *look how badly it wants to live.*"

"You guys seem to exist," I say. "You're both real."

"Tattoo my ass," says Precious. He reaches over Felix's head to turn on his TV, queuing up a series of videos of people filming themselves tattooing their own butts. Felix chugs the last of her borscht, pulls on a black rubber glove with a snap. Precious lifts two thumbs up, and then Felix does, and then I do it too. We sit there thumbs-upping each other. It is a thumbs-up standoff.

So our night passes like this: Felix tears three blank sheets out of her sketchbook and passes these around. She draws a horse, a series of tree stumps with mushrooms growing out of them, a snake, and a portrait of Precious. Precious draws several clams, some balloon animals, an axe, and a surprisingly convincing Paulie from *The Sopranos* smoking a cigar. I draw a portrait of Precious that morphs into a dog, a series of cubes, and a hole carved into what looks like the desert floor. Felix lies on her stomach. Precious draws cross-legged on the couch. I install some free trial version of Photoshop and draw on my laptop. Silence moves between us, punctuated by the sound of our next door neighbor, the one with the cat in the empty kitchen, who opens his window and blasts a Radiohead song into the small corridor between our buildings. I draw Saturn, a black hole, and several more cubes. Felix draws a bunch of rocks, or maybe they're teeth. The Radiohead singer goes *ooouuuuuuww* into the night. I can't see what Precious draws. Time passes, or it doesn't. It whisks through the room. It clots.

I bring my computer into bed and draw a fish with a butcher knife passing through its belly. I save my drawings and email them to Felix. I close my laptop and fall asleep. I dream that Girlfriend sprouts two additional heads. She comes up to the edge of her tank and undulates her three heads, rolling them in a circle, a spiral. She hisses a venom that emerges as a fine gas. The gas floats through the mesh roof of her tank and fills the whole room, which is magenta, bright magenta. I wake to the sound of Precious and Felix in the next room. Precious cries out like a little baby: *ooouuuuuuww*.

I fall asleep again. I wake and it's morning, time for work. Felix is gone. When I check my phone I see a photo of Precious's butt, a dark swelling guillotine smeared across its left cheek.

□ □ □

Reading: What is it? A line to the dead? One-sided participation in an endless conversation? And books, are these an archaic entertainment technology we keep around because we confuse the entertainment experience with the pursuit of knowledge? Or a trapdoor to the *ownership* of knowledge, the world's secret contents, its rights to property, its social contracts, its ultimately finite passages, available in print? You can buy books in bulk and use them to decorate your movie set or coffee shop, the same way a landowning dandy would decorate his personal study, organized by the color of the spine. These books can be blank inside, it doesn't matter.

Socrates says *don't read*, but then every successful communist revolution so far has been characterized by an organized push of workers into literacy. We know this sort of stuff, it comes to us through the available channels. We read about it.

Reading something on the page versus reading it onscreen—the eye's neutral landing upon inked-out text versus the constant strain of peering at a beam of light simulating paper. The different kinds of attention these exertions produce. Hannah lectures me about the bad example I set for staff when I read new stock at my standing desk for longer than a few minutes. What I learn is that I can read the same book, the same vibrating line to the dead, on my work computer and she'll say nothing, even if there's plenty of shipping or receiving to be done.

The way reading a print book violates the propriety of certain social settings via the intimate contact you make with it, bending over the baby-like book. Treating it with care. Turning a page. You don't incline over the computer. But then again I can whip out my phone and stare at that for the same duration of time it would take to read a few pages and Hannah doesn't care, and in this case the physical inclination—curved spine, cradling the thing in my hands—is identical.

The generous budget of time we allot a phone or computer in pretty much any circumstance versus the way a book seems almost to mock time, asking for time in a way we all agree is unacceptable.

The sense of *real reading* versus the way it happens on a device.

The perpetual snob-type assertion that real reading has vanished altogether. Even supposedly serious books aren't what they used to be. We don't sit cross-ankled in the dozing window seat overlooking a soundless bay as the low light passes over our blanketed knees and read that way for hours. Not anymore. Even if we did it wouldn't be the same.

I read the first twenty pages of a Gerald Murnane novel but find myself thinking about Felix instead. The sand in the air eroding her into an impossible shape. Her sense of the future. The image of the frictionless space jumps back into my head. A machine so well-oiled it runs by itself. I read a short story by Paul Scheerbart about a perpetual motion machine built to execute prisoners by carrying them off into the sky. A machine that comes together as it operates and then proceeds forever.

"No one answered my question before. Which is worse, slipping or being unable to slip? Being worn down in small ways, or feeling stuck, or carrying yourself off into the horizon?" I don't say this.

Hannah tells me that a million books are published every year, but then she says three million if we include self-published titles. I don't know what to believe. The total number of new books in the range of time between the first one ever published and the year 2010 is 130 million, apparently. If we count books after 2010 it could be double that. No one knows for sure. Books in the era of self-publishing become a matter of speculation, like dark matter or quarks: without question there exists another world, a world wrapped inside the one we see and feel, but we're unable to study its contours with any accuracy. You have to bounce light off the surface and see what reflects back. Hannah says that taken together the total amount of books ever published could stack its way to wherever, to the sun, Venus. A billion children's books per year. The industry shrinks, the industry is in crisis, the industry adapts. Audiobooks. The total amount of storage space to contain all those books must be at least a few million gigabytes. And on average a new book will attract a total of five readers, five ever, and then it will go away.

□ □ □

"A body without organs," says Precious. He's holding my copy of *Capitalism and Schizophrenia* over his head. For a second it looks like he's going to try balancing it on his nose like a seal.

"A body without organs," Felix repeats. She sketches a charcoal portrait of Precious, scribbling furiously as he cavorts around the apartment. Behind his head looms a guillotine.

"A body without *organs*." Precious is doing an opera singer's voice now, holding the word *organs* in a long stretch as he poses on a chair in the middle of the common room, hotdogging for an invisible audience.

"A body *without* organs," Felix screams. It's sharp and sudden enough for Precious to flinch himself off the chair.

"Smooth-brained."

"An egg."

"Like a baby, kind of."

"An excelsior body."

"Headless."

"Alright," I say.

"A *body* without organs." They say this together, facing me, Precious miming the grand gestures of a conductor closing down a symphony. Felix bursts into applause.

□ □ □

Now that I'm a manager I will sometimes interview potential booksellers with Hannah. "We have to find people who will stay through the off-season," she says. "Who have nowhere to go once it gets nice out."

Here's how it works. Every few days someone responds to the always-hiring ad at the bottom of the store's website—or, if they've had the fear of humiliation wrung out of them from past service industry jobs (*always a good sign*, says Hannah) they will simply walk up to the registers and hand their single-page resume to whoever's clocked in. If the applicant is especially good this moment will turn into a whole conversation.

Every Monday Hannah clicks through the company inbox for cold callers. She shuffles the stack of paper resumes. Promising ones, or notably awful ones, she passes to me. Someone has designed their resume to look like a bunch of fortunes coming out of fortune cookies. Someone has spent extra on thick paper and an embossed nameplate but only lists being a landlord. Aspiring DJs, private tutors, single moms. The youngest, richest-seeming applicants—anyone who lists a publication or an internship—Hannah will pass off to Ford, who almost always hires these people at the flagship.

What I learn is that there is a whole class of people who don't need to work but work anyway. Maybe this is specific to the region. But a particular type of person applies for a job in retail purely for the sake of having something to do. The moment-to-moment experience of work becomes a game to play, a warding-off of nuisances, a collection of trifles. Customers from hell. The art of catching counterfeit bills. Capital, I assume, accrues elsewhere.

An adult with a child's face walks into the store wearing a blue shirt and high pink shorts. He shakes our hands—firm, eye contact—as Hannah directs him to one of the sofa chairs in the corner of the sales floor. He seems to survey what is already his. We drag our stools over to meet him.

The interview begins. I describe the shift of an hourly staff worker, and then Hannah asks questions designed to raise red flags. "Shelving," I say. "A lot of quick transactions. Special orders. Our POS system is really old." The man-child intuits Hannah's authority over the proceedings and directs his blue gaze to her. "Recommendations," I say. "Someone will come up and ask you to produce a book they don't remember the name of. It's important to have a go-to title for every genre. *Publisher's Weekly*, the bestsellers lists. Some heavy lifting. A trial period then the union. We always need people who can work weekends." All this comes rolling out of me.

"What's your favorite book?" asks Hannah after I finish. The applicant uncrosses his legs and shifts his weight forward so that his elbows perch on his knees, fingers tented. Hannah and I both pull back a little in our seats. Mora, working the registers, looks over at us, concern passing over her face. The glass door at the shop's entrance opens by itself and a gust of wind follows. The man-child doesn't blink, nor does he break eye contact with Hannah. "*Blood Meridian*," he says.

Here are Hannah's red flags when assessing potential hires: no eye contact, no resume, a resume with over-embellished graphic design like the fortune cookie one, bad favorite book (it has to be very bad), *Blood Meridian* as favorite book, something she'll only call *trash aesthetic* and won't explain further, no answer to *what have you liked that has come out recently*, aggressive eye contact, inability to work weekends. Really, there is only one red flag, and that is having the wrong vibe. The interview process has more to do with assessing whether an applicant will at any point become violent—toward a customer, toward fellow staff, toward the architecture of the store itself—than it does with whether some stranger can perform an arbitrary chain of tasks. It is nothing to work a register, but doing so every day, in the company of others, this is another matter.

Maybe at a level beyond retail it becomes about competence, or pedigree. I don't know. Here the question of violence hovers over the entire process.

□ □ □

On the subway, a computerized voice reminds us that the police can conduct search and seizure of our belongings at any time. We are told to report suspicious behavior. We are told not to leave anything anywhere.

"Darling Precious," says Felix. "How is your ass feeling?"

"Good now. There were a few days where I wanted a new one." He sticks his butt out; we look at it. Blue jeans. "Pooping felt weird," he says.

We barrel downtown toward Glossy's restaurant. According to Precious this place will almost certainly go out of business soon, and the waitstaff has decided to treat its last few weeks as a kind of sustained party. We venture south to join the destruction.

In the evening a layer of ice cakes the city, and in the morning it thaws out again.

"What's crazy," says Felix, using my shoulders as an armrest and swaying against the train's current, "is that like eighty people have messaged me asking if I'll tattoo them. In one week. Every single one has specifically requested that I do their ass."

"On my end too," Precious says. "I'm getting a lot of comments, *where did you get your ass done,* even though you're clearly in the video. You're tagged and everything."

Here's what happened. The other night, after I fell asleep, Precious decided to turn Felix's tattooing practice into a full-on spectacle for his feed. Together they arranged Rompe Conjuros and Precious's other votives against a stage of improvised balloon torture devices (a balloon crucifix, a balloon axe, balloon stockades) as well as a perpetual downward stream of bubbles and confetti. The video begins with this spill. Then, from the bottom of the frame, Precious's ass, abstracted in its sudden appearance, rises to the tempo of a C-Pop song Glossy played for us a couple weeks ago, whereupon it is struck from above by a tattoo needle in the grip of a gloved pair of disembodied hands. *Ow*, says Precious, *Jesus*. Then cut, closeup on his left cheek and the beginnings of a blue-black mass welting over it. Felix is singing along with the song, and you can just make out Precious's low whimpering. He sounds like a puppy. Cut again, this time to the song's glimmering climax. There's his whole ass, legible for the first time as such, with its new guillotine smack in the center of the left cheek, receding into an ever greater swell of glitter and bubbles, foam and smoke, as the music crescendos and detritus overtakes the screen. Thirteen seconds total. "It's cheap," Precious explains on the train, "it's pandering. But it's doing numbers."

"I'm a little worried about becoming the ass tattoo guy," says Felix. "Yesterday I did three in a row, three friends, out in Queens. One of them was telling me about how they were heading to a club later that night where you have to pass an interview before they'll let you in. This club gauges how cool you are, and the interview is full of trick questions. But then she said she had found a leak of the interview online and that she was memorizing the best answers." She shakes her head. "They'll let anyone get a tattoo these days."

"If you do any more nearby let me know," says Precious. "Could turn our video into a whole series."

It has begun lately to feel like there's no end to the city. There's more city beyond the city, and beyond that too. I walk around with the suspicion that everything is a city. The internet, for example, is a sprawling, scrambled-out city. But trees are also cities if you look close enough. A single branch is a city for moss, ants, bees, mushrooms. A mushroom is itself a city. The body a city. My eyes close.

Expanding and expanding. The distance that has opened between me and Felix since karaoke night. Inertia and entropy.

The problem again asserts itself. What is work? What are our days for?

What happens when you are trapped?

What am I? Do I want Felix's attention, or do I want to be Felix?

"Some kid is offering to drive me out to the Hamptons," she says. "Specifically for her butt. I got an inquiry from someone in Sweden this morning. I don't understand what's going on."

"That's fame, baby," Precious says.

This is an important announcement from the New York City Police Department, says the voice from the subway's ceiling.

□ □ □

A city of individuated human bodies blocks the entrance to Glossy's restaurant. We add to the crush, Felix slipping through the negative space between shoulders and Precious producing a natural part in the crowd with his broad steps.

At the front, we find Glossy on the restaurant phone, talking faster than I've ever heard anyone speak before while engaging in a simultaneous encounter made up of rapid gestures and hand signals with a bald man who looks furious not to have already been seated. Then, still producing language into the phone—"you have my full assurance that while I completely understand and even share your frustration about this setback I am still unfortunately not able to take any more reservations tonight and there is as I've already explained quite a long and growing line for tables currently so as I've said we will only be able to seat you when your entire party arrives yes your entire party including your brother yes even though he's not responding to your texts I do certainly understand that that's inconvenient"—using just her eyes and flaring nostrils she greets us, wordlessly communicates her desire to be dead or least drunk, and with a slight tilt of the head sends us outside to wait. She conveys the bald man to a table at the restaurant's dark stern.

Yellow neon lights frame the restaurant's front window, casting a shift of orange over the various eaters. Music blares. "Let's go," Precious says. We wait outside.

"Deep in the fucking weeds," says Glossy an hour later when we're finally seated. She distributes three deep red micheladas from her tray and plants a metal straw in each one. We toast to her—she curtsies—and drink. A cloud of steam emerges from the square aperture between the dining room and the kitchen, a white steam tinting green. "One of our cooks almost blinded himself earlier tonight," Glossy says. "It's probably a hundred fifty degrees back there. We're like an hour behind." She adjusts her bra. "But I'll walk out of here with several hundred dollars in cash, and then this entire place will just disappear. Poof!"

Precious waves this information away, bringing his drink to Glossy's lips. Another hour later we've almost finished our massive plates of shrimp bulgogi, making a game out of observing Glossy's changing face as she interacts with every other person in the room. Which mask will she wear at this particular moment, to fit the needs of this one member of the public? What about this one?

"She's the opposite of you," Felix says as Precious burps. "When you work you're like a French waiter in a movie. Leaning away from people, nose in the air. Now watch her." Across the room Glossy inclines into a woman's face, ear to mouth. She writes something in a scratchpad and touches the woman's shoulder, then seems to recite a long list, shaking her head *no* as though to punctuate whatever she's saying. Her smile, already wide, grows as she talks.

"She'd be a good clown," says Precious. Now Glossy balances five or six bottles of wine on a single tray and carries this to a table of five or six people. "Look at her eyes though. She's splitting open."

"Service," I say. "I don't know how you deal with it."

"Service," says Felix. She fishes the lime out of her michelada. "Going to restaurants because you love to be waited on. You love receiving service. The feeling of it."

Precious burps again. "I think culinary school is killing my love of eating," he says.

"What am I thinking of," I say, drawing a blank. "The something. The dialectic. About service."

"Squid," says Glossy. She's at the table next to ours now, scribbling into her little scratchpad. "Egg. Shellfish." I catch my reflection in the buzzing yellow window.

"Folks," says Felix. Where did she pick that up?

"I can literally taste every corner they're cutting here. I could list the ingredients they swapped out for something cheaper." Precious pushes his bulgogi away and mimes flipping the whole table over. "They're rushing this shit."

"Public service," says Felix. "Protect and serve."

"One person needs the other person to not exist in order to exist," I say. "What is that called?"

"Vegan, sure," says Glossy. "Gluten, yes. Lots of gluten."

"It's a fantasy place," says Felix. "The restaurant. Right? It doesn't exist."

"Nearly blinding yourself though."

"And daikon. Daikon? A radish."

"But that's hidden. At the front it's Glossy."

"Performing service."

"Aestheticizing labor. Is that a word? Making it sexy."

"What is a radish? As in like, what are radishes?"

"No, no," says Precious. He makes a buzzer sound. "Completely wrong. Both of you. Wrong again."

□ □ □

The distance from the sister location to our apartment is forty blocks. Forty blocks, or two and a half miles, a forty-five minute walk if I move the whole time and in a straight shot. If I take the long way by the river it's closer to an hour.

The old man calls as I'm leaving. My coat vibrates against the wind. He wants to know if I've found a new apartment yet. "Weren't you going to leave?" he says. "Have you checked listings closer to where you work? I hear prices go down when it gets cold. Is it still cold out there? Now that you've gotten a raise, can't you live alone? Don't you want your own place? What? What?"

The wind from the river finds its way down the neck of my shirt. "We're trying," I say into the phone, cupping it against my mouth. "We found a realtor. It's hard out here."

Felix bought us a plug-in induction stove, which boils water in thirty seconds and has two full burners. It lives on top of the non-functional gas range. The unit next door remains vacant. The construction resumes, stops again, moves to other floors. Eventually our roof will collapse or workers will come and install a load-bearing beam. Precious learns that the CEO of the company that owns our building has been convicted for murder, or has been murdered, I don't bother to internalize which it is. Someday the entire city will be reduced to rubble—we labor under the condition that we will die.

A law is something beneath which one is subject. It happens regardless of the subject paying it any attention. In the lawless microcosm of our brick building next to the elevated train, a shell company headed by either a murderer or a ghost sanctions illegal construction and ignores the failure of basic utilities, and we with equal disregard for the rules withhold our rent. We haven't paid since December.

"You haven't what?" says the old man. I realize, walking, that I forgot to unclip my boxcutter from my belt. "Listen," he says. "How is everything going," a pause, "emotionally?"

Something I've noticed not just in myself but with everyone in the city around this time of year is that there's a swell of almost violent energy that tears through cold days in particular. The wind blows in from both rivers at once, funneling down the city grid. The sun flirts but doesn't reveal itself. People get aggressive. And then, when the sun does come out, a manic release of bodies from their apartments and clothes. The bookstore, right next to the park, fills with shoppers furious in their jubilance, and then it empties again. The same way the murder rate spikes around the full moon. If it were acceptable to stage cock fights in public there'd be a ring in every patch of sunlight. Wailing strangers clutching their dollar bills. I'd be in there too.

I walk into a beam of sunlight, tear open my coat, and repress the urge to throw my phone into the Hudson. I throw the boxcutter instead.

□ □ □

Something happens. Precious has me and Glossy meet him at a bar in the basement of a Lebanese restaurant and orders a round of arak with mint tea before explaining what it is. Then he presents his right hand, which had been resting on his lap: wrapped in a blue cast, purple fingers poking out of the gauze like sausages, little piggies. Glossy gasps, her own hands shooting to her mouth.

"When did this happen?" I ask.

"This morning." Precious blows on his tea. "My boss was driving me and five other clowns in this van he just bought. No seats in the back. We were huddled back there with the helium tanks and costumes." He takes a sip. "He wound up rear-ending the car in front of us on the highway. Me and the other clowns went flying. Crunched my hand on the landing."

Glossy, who started smiling the moment Precious demonstrated his cast, has cracked in half with mirth. "Time for a lawyer." She almost spits this. "Time to organize."

"Are the other clowns okay?" I ask.

"Get written testimonies from everyone in the car." Glossy slams her fist on the table. "You're getting paid."

"I'm quitting," Precious says. "Everyone was high at the time, including me. They're fine. I don't think the person we hit even had a license."

"Clusterfuck," I say.

"It's just a fracture. I'll get a marker so you guys can sign the cast."

"Hospitals."

"I mostly feel lucky the helium tanks didn't explode."

"Unacceptable," Glossy shouts, pushing back in her seat and stomping up to the bar.

My spine trembles. Precious and I sit in silence.

Precious. In his blue cast, sitting there. His hair curling past his shoulders, his fraying jean jacket, his eyes wrapped in skull. Felix once showed me a slideshow of dogs who look like their owners: two faces that slide into definition until they become the same. I wonder if Precious grows to resemble me or I him. Which of us is the dog? He scratches his cast, exhales, and then uses a butter knife to scratch the skin under his cast.

Glossy returns with a full mezze plate: pickles, hummus, labneh, bread. "Unacceptable," she says again. "What about finals?"

"I mean, it's my right hand, so my knife skills are fucked. Kneading dough will be impossible. Do you think they'll give me an extension?"

"You guys have finals?" I ask.

"Ten dishes in five days. It's mostly easy stuff." He reaches for a pickle with his right hand, dipping his cast into a density of hummus. He tries again with the left.

"I don't think it'll be easy," says Glossy. "We have to make this duck pâté thing, inside a pastry. Takes days. Maybe they'll let me sous for you?"

"We can practice together." Precious dabs at his hummus-caked cast with a napkin. "Someone probably makes a one-handed rolling pin. Or I could fuse a knife to my cast somehow. Like a sword arm."

Glossy holds the cast, measuring its weight. We eat without talking. Then Precious sighs. "It's not even interesting anymore, clowning," he says. "Other than going to a really rich person's house. You go off script and the parents get upset. You get too weird and the kids freak out. Then there's the animal abuse."

"The racism," says Glossy.

"For a while I was kind of fascinated by how gross it all was. You know." He gestures around the restaurant with a butter knife. "It felt important almost. Doing this weird show all over town. Felt like I was learning something about how entertainment works." He brightens. "And who wants it, and what they do with it once they have it. Kids get almost pissed off when they're entertained for too long. Nothing happens when you hit the upper limit. I created a few kid mosh pits during my routine, just so they could try getting it all out. But I don't think catharsis actually helps. That's one thing clowning taught me." He regards his tea. "Anyway. Routine set in. I think I can go a month or two without needing work."

"But if you move," says Glossy.

"If we move." He looks at me. "And if our murderer comes after us about rent. I honestly have no idea."

"You could come work at the bookstore," I say, struck by the fact that I never had the thought before. "There's no actual work to do currently. It's only getting slower. Your broken hand wouldn't matter." What I don't say is that his presence would cut through the workday's sludge as if by magic. He and I would form a unified front, a shared reality superseding whatever logic the bookstore weaves over a nine-hour shift, such that the possibilities for real personhood would avail themselves to me in a way I never allowed myself to fantasize about before, or at least not on the job.

One thing about Precious that I've noticed in the almost-year of living with him one-on-one is the speed with which he rolls bad news into a kind of performance. The saw flashing through the wall of our living room, the patch of ice on the highway—the distance he creates between himself and the object of his ire, or fear. He pulls the same face now that he did those times.

A pause.

"You are always puking and falling asleep," he says finally. A real frown passes over his face. "Look what they did to you."

He looks at his phone as I feel mine buzz. Felix has group-messaged a series of emojis suggesting that she's off tattooing someone and wishes she could have joined us for tea.

Precious replies with a gif of a dog puking then licking its puke back up. He's been using this as a response to everything lately.

I text the word *it's* and let my phone autocomplete the rest: *it's not a problem at all the time I get to work on the phone with my apartment is weird.*

We truck in unintelligibility, these days, I guess.

"I'll work at your store," says Glossy. I look up from my phone. "I don't care about any of that stuff. I need a job."

My phone buzzes again. *Is your butt hacked*, Felix texts. Precious sends a different gif of the same dog puking and eating its puke. *How many of those do you have*, says Felix.

□ □ □

At the bookstore, to shut me up, Hannah says her secret is that she's able to turn herself off for forty hours per week. "It's the only way I get through," she says. "Autopilot." Rearranging display pieces, shuffling the locations of various sections by genre, compiling staff schedules for the forthcoming week, answering Ford's many emails, shelving, reminding staff to go on their fifteen-minute breaks, and then also working the registers, responding to queries on the phone and in person, checking for counterfeit bills, managing customer returns for cash or store credit, asking if any given customer is a member of the store's loyalty program while bagging their purchases in the store's branded paper bags and signing them up for the program if they don't mind providing their name and email address. "When I go home I get to use my brain again," she says. "It's fine." Then she tells me to go on a fifteen-minute break.

Ford walks up with a balsa wood skeleton of a stegosaurus the size of a small horse. "Where should we put this?" he says. Without responding, Hannah carries the model downstairs to the Kids Section.

Ford paces up and down the sales floor. A customer or two noses through the bestsellers, but otherwise the store becomes Ford-centric. Light bends around him. He says *hello* in a menacing voice to a woman pushing through the front doors. I change the store's music to a single repeating Philip Glass song. He studies the new nonfiction display. "Penguin Random House," he says finally. He warps his way behind the registers and observes the day's receiving load, stacked against my standing desk: four boxes from Harper, three from Hachette, and a single brown envelope from Scholastic. "This is all you have," says Ford. "Where is everything else?"

Here is a bookselling term I learned recently: *on hold*. When the store is put on hold, this means Ford's line of credit has dipped below zero and the major publisher-distributors refuse to send us any more cargo until he's made the requisite back payments. Incoming shipments dwindle. I stare at Ford's chin. All the bestsellers feature magenta covers behind thick white font. The Philip Glass song sounds like thought overturning.

"One reason for the freeze is we're not processing returns fast enough," he says, standing next to me now. "Can you get a Penguin return in the pipeline?"

I study the pores on his chin. The deep craters between his eyebrows. Then something interesting happens. The store's vegan leather purses, the clear blue and magenta plastic knife sets, the enormous feather lamps sold at a dilated markup—I watch as all of it closes in on Ford's body, and not just his body, but his whole quivering being, his moving sharklike through the world: the store's material shrinks around him, corrals him in place, until he's stuck, buglike, a postcard-sized oil painting dwarfed by the massive, cracked, gilded frame surrounding it.

□ □ □

When I get home I find Glossy hovering behind Precious as he attempts to chop an onion. He has crammed the hilt of his longest knife deep into his cast, fingers wrapped around the lowermost part of its blade. Glossy stands on her toes, hands out. Neither of them seem to be breathing.

My entering breaks the spell. The knife pushes rather than cuts through the onion, sending it bouncing across the cutting board and into the sink. Glossy gasps. Precious grimaces in pain.

"Guess I'll go kill myself," he says, tearing the knife out of his cast and throwing it into the sink to join the onion.

When Precious storms out of the kitchen Glossy does the thing where she rolls her eyes and dances, pretend-grinding against the space Precious left behind. "He'll survive," she says.

□ □ □

Nothing comes together. I try to read Michel Houellebecq but get so nauseous and bored I have to stop. I try reading *The Maximus Poems*. I try reading *Gender Trouble*. I try reading *The Queer Art of*

Failure. I try Knausgaard but get bored again. I try reading *A Little Life*. I try reading *The Geography of the Imagination*. I try reading *The Poetics of Space*. I try reading *Hopscotch*. I try reading Robert Coover, then John Cheever, looking for a line across the two authors that doesn't exist. I try reading Ishiguro.

Who makes this shit? How does anyone get a single thing done?

"New York is starting to feel like a bunch of restaurants," says Felix.

"Socialism is an outfit you see people wearing on weekends," says Glossy.

"This is how you're supposed to eat it," says Precious, taking a big bite out of an orange like it's an apple.

□ □ □

The bookstore stays on hold. My daily receiving load dwindles to basically nothing.

Antoine shuttles in a single box on his UPS hand truck and performs a pantomime of lifting it onto my standing desk as though it were extremely heavy, wiping his brow before scanning the barcode and asking me to sign. "What do you do with yourself all day?" he says.

Here's what I do: I purchase industrial quantities of toilet paper from a thousand-page wholesale catalog. I flip the catalog open and buy everyone on staff a new retractable boxcutter that looks and functions like a switchblade. I buy a double-thickness rubber mat for behind the registers. Unbleached paper towels and vacuum-sealed bags of antibacterial soap. Several hundred rolls of receipt paper and price tags. I buy packing tape. I'm redirected to a special FREE OFFERS page just before checkout. Objects of oddly high quality, tiered by price-point—today's order, just shy of a thousand dollars, has me decide between a ceramic knife set for Precious and an elaborate toolbox that could double as a container for art supplies for Felix. Or a wool and felt camouflage blanket with an elk's head rendered lovingly in its center, for me. It looks fake, it looks real. I click it.

That's one day. On the next the supplies arrive and I spend hours reorganizing the storage area downstairs, making space for the rolls of toilet paper. I refill the paper towel dispensers in the store's two bathrooms and draw a little diagram explaining how to refill these so there isn't always a roll congealing into an unusable wet mass next to the sink. I refill the soap dispensers. I unroll the rubber mat behind the registers and design a system for storing receipt paper, and then I go through all the old files on my computer until I find a document full of passwords to various email addresses, killing hours reading conversations between past receiving managers and Ford. I go several years back, describing a lineage of managers all the way to the store's opening. No one lasts longer than a year. I wrap myself in my new wool and felt blanket as I exit the store, walking into the windy night, elk's face squared between my shoulder blades.

One day Hannah has me manage the store's social media accounts, but I'm so bad at it she changes the account's password after a few posts.

We begin to miss important books. The Pulitzer is announced but the store has none of the finalists in stock, just a single copy of the winning novel, which someone buys within hours of the announcement. This book in particular becomes an ongoing thing. A consistent meter of customers come to the store impatient to have already read it, so Ford instructs staff to imply that we just happened to sell our last copy of that particular book but have placed an order with the distributor for dozens more copies, and that while it's always a tight market for an award-winning book after a major prize announcement (usually the publisher rushes a new print run to keep up with demand) we will let the customer know the moment more copies arrive, especially if they buy it in advance. This is all theoretically true. But then weeks pass, and it becomes impossible not to recognize the returning faces of those who have already paid for this book, who have since watched it morph into a cultural phenomenon and want to know why they don't yet own it. Eventually Ford lugs in three Amazon boxes full of this one book and we spend the rest of the day calling customers to inform them that their order is in, though they have in the meantime also turned to Amazon. "No refunds," says Ford. "Store credit only."

During a managers-only meeting he says *the best way to move forward is to keep staff in the dark about the hold*, though it's obvious to everyone that the shelves are thinning. There's nothing to do. You would just have to walk in and look around.

One day, miraculously, a pipe bursts in the Kids Section and floods the whole bottom floor. A thick ochre grease lines the walls. I spend hours wading through the knee-high water wearing long rubber boots I bought from Basics Plus using the store's petty cash, calling plumbers, taking videos of the wreckage and sending these to Hannah and Ford in one text thread and Precious, Glossy, and Felix in another—videos of, for example, plastic buckets full of handwoven dolls from Lithuania sailing across a grease and water sea from one end of the Kids Section to the other, or the burst pipe directly above the downstairs registers pouring grease onto the computer's keyboard. I spend hours salvaging stock that hasn't yet submerged, anything near the splash zone that doesn't stink I bring to the second floor, and then, after the plumbers manage to turn the water off, I start the long bailing-out process, carrying plastic buckets of burnt rubber-smelling water away from the Kids Section, down the break room hallway, and out into the alleyway behind the store, opening a manhole with a crowbar from Basics Plus and dumping the filthy water down the black aperture, into the unknown, hearing it land with a thunk rather than a splash onto whatever's down there. In the days to come I will continue salvaging stock, ripping out the engorged carpeting, cleaning and eventually painting over the greasy walls. The toilet paper, the many boxes of brown paper towels, all of it destroyed. I leave the store bursting with energy. Felix and I hold each other in the moonlight, my body flush with an exhaustion that feels somehow like nourishment. The two different frequencies of our bodies momentarily sync up. It's tremulous, wobbling, but we are together. Problems and solutions. I wake up and set off to work.

□ □ □

Felix's nascent online fame has turned into a genuine phenomenon. Some internet celebrity flies her to Los Angeles to tattoo his famous butt. That's where she is now.

She asks me to housesit. I cross Harlem by foot and open the front door of her building using the blue key. With the silver key I open her unit's door, and then I jam the handle back into its place so it locks. Already it smells different. I fall asleep on her foldout couch-bed and wake up seven hours later. I open the blinds in every room and pace around, boiling water for coffee. I talk to myself. The floorboards creak.

Felix's apartment overlooks a broad street lined with trees. April sprigs, lined-up bundles of lace. I sit on the floor and pour coffee into a handmade ceramic mug, probably one of Felix's creations. I turn on the lights and turn them off again. This time of year you choose between a lightbulb's wan yellow and the window's underwater glow. I click on the conical heat lamp at the top of Girlfriend's glass tank and the room washes in scarlet. The shadows disappear. Girlfriend peeks out from under an oblong strip of bark. She smells with her tongue.

I fold Felix's bed into a couch and stare at the red-bathed snake. Everything in her room is kept as close to the floor as possible:

In lieu of a bookshelf, she stacks her books in knee-high piles on either side of the snake tank, a small mountain range penning in the dragon. She has stacked them spine-in, identifying information facing the wall. An anonymous pile of pages.

Felix. Dear reader, I have failed to describe her to you. Her smell. Her laugh and perpetually stained shirts. The outpouring of art objects that emerge from her bedroom in the middle of the night. Where do you even go to fire ceramic in Manhattan? The paintings on wood panels, the family portrait she made of the three of us with a single line, a complete likeness, making it look like we've been carved into a mountainside.

We have known each other for less than a year. We met by chance on an ordinary day and continued to talk, first texting, then calling, then meeting in parks, the stoop of her building. Something inarticulable has grown out of these everyday events.

Phe-nom-e-no-log-i-cal.

When the next thing happens, whatever it is, I want it to be with Felix. Leaving the city or never leaving it. Finding a life for ourselves or never finding it.

I stuff Felix's keys into my pocket and am out the door, down the stairs. I walk south toward the thin park. Nothing in particular comes to mind. Seeing without vision. What strategies does an author, any author, have at their disposal to describe other people? Especially those so close they become hard to see? How to describe your own smell?

◻ ◻ ◻

And what about the snake? I return to Felix's room and resume staring at her. She slithered to the other side of her tank in my absence, but now that I'm here again she doesn't move.

We stare at each other. In the room's silence I realize I haven't been alone, really alone, in weeks.

My back releases a blank, staccato pain that flits up and down the spine, a hand on the piano practicing scales.

It occurs to me that if you took my chronic pain, Felix's trailing perfume, Precious's fixation on taste, Girlfriend's unyielding stare, and the sound of Glossy's scraped-out voice you would have one complete, shambling body.

One of us, I think it was Precious, came up with the project. The project was: What if we, the three of us, or four of us now including Glossy, what if we recorded the most ordinary moments from our nothing-industry jobs in such a way that centered on their absurdity? And then what if we laid these beside one another, floated each pearl along the same line? A video series, or a website, or poems. Call them work songs. A kind of game we play, throwing our jobs at each other, rifling through them, looking for the hidden places where meaning is stored. Sand through fingers. Getting worked up about some detail, or the buildup of pressure that comes with a few normal elements piled atop one another: time, boredom, underpay. The body. We already do this all the time. *But what if we formalized the process*, asked one of us.

"Still," I say now to the empty room.

Still, though: Why fixate on all this, actually? In real life? Why this way?

Obliteration and ruin, retail workers, service workers. Humiliation carried around and carried home. Minutiae and ritual. The question being *what happens to a person pressed against the glass?*

The hospital bills for a broken wrist Precious will either attempt to pay with a crowdsourced fundraiser online or won't.

The top surgery one of us will have or has already had, I won't say which. The arcing need for gender realignment shared in a spectrum pushing deep into red. Our made up names.

With a state of affairs such as these, in a planet full of creatures such as this captive snake in her glass tank, who looks at me but doesn't blink.

■ ■ ■

Let me tell you. Snakes lose their front legs first, sometime in the Cretaceous. In England we find fossils of half-snake half-lizards, one hundred seventy million years old, riding around on their long bellies and dwindling hind legs. Pythons and boas (the oldest snakes) retain traces of back legs in the form of tiny hooks used to this day to latch onto mates during sex. They evolve slowly, they evolve everywhere, they spread across the planet. The specialized snake. Burrowing through any collection of rocks and pulling out a rat or an egg. The quick getaway. The snake that darts into freshwater and whips its way across. Sidewinding over sand, constricting its way through kudzu. They burn through the ages without a long enough ribcage—their bodies extend past it, growing tails that eventually take on muscle. Their organs squeeze through a new body. The lungs flatten and stretch themselves into place. Geographical preference and slow branching-off selection: snakes whose venom only kills birds, and then only specific birds. A coiled mangrove snake flinging itself face-first off a branch and into the sky, seizing a sand martin in its jaw, paralyzing it instantly, and falling ropelike on a bed of decaying leaves. The bird twitching down its throat. The snake becoming more and more of a secret. Millions of years pass. The snake's hidden fangs, hidden hemipenes, the cobra's retractable hood. A tail that vibrates at a rate of fifty pulses per second, and then this tail hollows out (millions more years pass) into a series of interlocked keratin cells that slam against each other so loudly it silences every other creature in its vicinity. Snake music.

And then of course the human reaction to a world full of snakes. The image of a coiled snake with the sudden spear—knife, buckshot, hatchet—shot through it. Precious and I watch an episode of *The Sopranos* where Tony and Paulie watch a documentary about snakes. Later in the episode Tony has sex next to a glassed-off snake terrarium as a twelve foot boa looks on. All the misattribution. Snakes named after anything other than the snake itself: corn snake, rat snake, bull snake, chicken snake, cat snake, eyelash viper, ball python, fox snake, milk snake, children's python, tiger snake, wart snake, snorkel viper. Baby-faced humans peering behind glass, making lists. Naturally I contribute to this lineage. Even Felix, who can't articulate what drew her to Girlfriend in the first place, has some hand in all this.

Girlfriend as a fragment of deep time. A living thread, imbricated within an invisible continuity that simply occurs. Is any of this coming through? I wander around Felix's kitchen and microwave some frozen tamales. I pour hot water into her ceramic mug and add whiskey. I find a wedge of lemon and some green salsa in the fridge door. The former I squeeze into my drink and the latter I pour over my tamales. Now I'm back on her couch, watching the red glass cube with a snake in it, still buzzing with thoughts peeling off me like steam. I write the thoughts down.

◻ ◻ ◻

I dream Girlfriend is twelve feet tall and a hundred feet wide, so I step into her the way you step into a subway car. I dream she's a shadow passing over the moon, or she's the moon itself shattering over Manhattan, burying everything in debris. She's a balloon animal twisting into words I can't read. I wake and Felix's room glows red. The real Girlfriend flattens herself against the glass of her tank, inching around like a worm.

◻ ◻ ◻

My body reiterates its regular functioning. I purchase the same two bananas for fifty cents from the fruit cart down the block, prepare the same coffee in the break room urn downstairs. The store still smells like grease from the flood, and we have slowed to almost complete stillness.

Hannah sifts through her weekly stack of resumes. I scroll through job listings online.

A lab downtown that analyzes ripped-out carpet samples for asbestos, receiving manager needed. Art handling and logistics on a gig basis for galleries like Felix's. Graveyard shift at a luxury dog hotel. Crew member at Trader Joe's, truck loader for UPS, dishwasher, barback, runner, associate, clerk, personal assistant, intern, driver, private tutor, independent contractor, social media manager, call center care provider.

Hannah finds Glossy's resume in the pile. "Not terrible," she says, passing the page over to me. "Service industry. The organizing might raise an eyebrow with Ford. Did you ever eat there?" She points to the name of Glossy's restaurant. "I read an amazing review of this place, and then it just vanished."

□ □ □

Glossy sits cross-legged on the sofa chair in the sales floor corner. She wears a dress and lipstick, something I've never seen her do before. A silk scarf covers the tattoo on her clavicle, which is the full phrase WHAT IS TO BE DONE?

Hannah and I drag over our stools. The interview begins. "The off-season," I say. "But also the Christmas rush. The Christmas bonus. I know winter seems far away, but we need staff who can long-haul it." I think about Mora downstairs, who is at this moment doing one of the weekly story-time read-alongs, where a puddle of toddlers point at the picture book chosen by Mora to read in her best children-forward voice. Then I hear Ford's regular voice: *a public service, folks, a public service.* "The Kids Section in particular," I say. "You have to be able to navigate parents. Also nannies." Glossy produces a functional smile. "Shelving," I say. "We always need people who can work weekends."

"What's your favorite book?" Hannah asks when I finish. The ouroboros makes a complete turn. How many times have we done this? I hold my gaze on the patch of skin between Glossy's eyes, forgetting for a moment that we scripted this part out at the Lebanese restaurant.

"If I'm being honest, probably *Mrs. Dalloway*," she says. Her posture is perfect, I realize. "I know that's not a very interesting choice. Right now I'm reading *Malina* though, and that's kind of blowing my mind. I'm in my isolated women narrators having violent and obsessive reactions to male dominated social structures era."

Glossy does read—she has her own, actual favorite books. I forget what she said these were. Still, I thought it made sense to feed her the most correct possible answers to Hannah's questions. Her posture sends it over the edge. The look on Hannah's face now is that of someone who has just been informed of their eligibility for a large cash settlement, the compensation for an unnamed and deep-burning grievance. "*Malina*," she whispers.

◻ ◻ ◻

Glossy hooks her arm into mine as we slow-walk around the sales floor. I point out stock locations and note the store's organizational system. We travel downstairs to the Kids Section and breathe in the residual stench from the grease flood. Mora says something. I respond with something else.

The whole shop seems to change under Glossy's scrutiny. It's like she's a funhouse mirror, or a disco ball, refracting the various rooms back to themselves. The layers of grime on the windows, the way dust travels from the vents in the ceiling into compacted strata in corners of the floor. Also the hyper-focused lights that leave behind an uncanny absence of shadows. The spotlights on specialty products, the store's reflection in the grimy windows after the sun sets. Blue but also orange.

It looks as bad as it is: a bookstore without books. I try apologizing for the general state of things. "Not a ton of integrity," I say.

Glossy stops in her tracks and puts a hand on my shoulder. "Listen," she says. "The owner of my old restaurant withheld wages from a good two-thirds of kitchen staff because they were undocumented. He implied more than once that I'd get the schedule I wanted if I let him watch me change." She looks around. "A low integrity bookstore, that's fine. It's ideal."

We push through the back door into the alleyway between the store and the restaurant next door, a flood of noise following us. "Thanks for this," she says. A bird lands on the fire escape above us, mashing its head against a corner of metal. A jackhammer sound starts up. My new friend Glossy. We stand there like two kids.

□ □ □

Now I will describe our apartment at this stage of its life cycle.

Someone has reinforced the hole in the ceiling with what looks like a split-open trash bag. It expands and contracts with the wind. We vacuum the accumulated pools of drywall from the corner of every room. The gashes left by saws in the common room wall we cover with three layers of blue-white eggshell paint. The color lends a certain dimension to the apartment; *prestige*, Felix calls it when she returns from Los Angeles. Precious brings home a detail of cleaning products so we spend a weekend scraping grime off the molding and windowsills.

The light changes with the changing season. Precious drives to West Virginia for his grandmother's birthday and comes back with a realist painting he made in high school of a plate of steak and eggs. We hang this over the common room table. Our couch, the smallest one we could find at IKEA, slumps forward. Glamdring, Gandalf's sword, finds a holster in the form of two taxidermy deer hooves Precious found at an estate sale—the sword hung not horizontally, like a rifle in a hunting lodge, but vertically, as in one of Felix's tarot cards, over the couch. The four of swords. Felix calls this gesture *ominous* and *impossible* and never sits on the couch for long. I am constantly falling asleep beneath the tip of Glamdring's blade.

My bedroom becomes a repository for paper objects. Tea lights, lithograph prints, a calendar for The Year of the Snake 1989 that I find at Goodwill. Felix's rolled-up drawings, her portraits of Precious, sumi ink exercises, still lifes. Whatever doesn't fit in her apartment twenty blocks north. My single bookshelf full of damaged or stolen stock. A growing stack of advance review copies next to the bed on its wood pallet. The napkin drawing of two penises snaked together that Felix brought from London. An acoustic guitar that appeared out of nowhere, which neither Precious nor I can remember bringing home. The view from my bed, the empty cubes of the other apartments.

Then there's Precious's bedroom, behind its three-quarters closed door. I never go in. The kitchen with its jars of pickled eggs and moonshine he brings back from West Virginia with the realist steak painting. Every cabinet brimming with industrial-sized bags of angel hair pasta, gallon tubs of olive oil, minute quantities of saffron and fennel pollen in glass containers. Novelty candy cereal express-mailed from Korea, flavorless gum, a half-empty pack of cigarettes. A peach with a bite taken out, three or four fruit flies living in the crater. An array of extremely sharp knives and a drawing of an angry serrated knife (the serrations are its teeth) captioned DRY ME ALL THE WAY. One or two rats for Girlfriend in back of the freezer grizzled with frost.

The nonfunctional gas stove, the radiator that becomes a stuttering faucet, the ceiling that sags, the shower with the head ripped off, the cracked bathroom tile. On the other hand we're too high up for rats, too insulated for roaches, and completely without neighbors unless you count the guy who lives in the building across the gap. Precious screens movies with the sound turned all the way up. When it's nice out we'll sit on the fire escape.

Today he's watching cooking shows from under a collapsing mound of blankets. "What I don't understand," he says, gesturing at the screen with his blue cast, "is the link between food prep and humiliation. It's the same at school. We were making eclairs, during finals, and everyone else finished with their choux pastry like fifteen minutes before me. They didn't give me an extension or let anyone help." He wipes his nose against the broad end of the cast. "I had to figure certain shit out on the fly, like how to beat an egg with one hand and pour flour with the other. At one point I stuck a rolling pin into my cast and started using that. I definitely aggravated the fracture applying pressure to it. Anyway," he says, "I was the last one doing anything in this massive, completely silent kitchen. Just going at it. I could feel everyone watching me. It felt like I was going to be taken out back and mercy killed." He mutes the TV, looks at me, then unmutes it again. "My question is this. Does that humiliated feeling exist because of cooking shows, like were we playing out a scene from TV, or do these shows only exist because that's how kitchens actually are? I still don't get it." On the screen, someone breaks into sobs as they describe the eggs in their hollandaise congealing over a too-hot fire. My stomach growls loud enough for Precious to mute the TV again and look.

This has been the routine since he failed his exams: I leave the apartment at seven, stand at my desk beside the registers as the store empties around me, and return home to find him watching cooking shows. The hospital bill for his broken arm—several loose sheets with a new set of calculations at the bottom each page, culminating in the red, pre-circled figure of *three thousand five hundred and twelve dollars*—remains open on the common room table, a black hole around which the rest of the apartment seems to revolve. Some days I come home and the apartment seems empty, but then a toilet flushes or I hear Precious shuffling around his bedroom. Other days I'll chop garlic and onions and he'll simmer a coconut fish curry for several hours, getting off the couch to stir the pot with his good hand, filling the apartment with the smell of galangal and fat, sea air and fruit, and then carrying the steaming bowls back to the slumped-over couch with its puke stain on the left cushion so we can eat in front of the TV.

◻ ◻ ◻

Bare reporting of facts. I no longer ship or receive books. Antoine stands on the curb outside the storefront, his hand truck empty. "Money," he calls, and then without waiting for a reply he pantomimes lifting something heavy above his head and hurling whatever the thing is supposed to be back onto the pavement. Without observing my reaction he returns to his truck, wiping the pretend sweat off his brow.

Today it's me and Glossy. I'm supposed to train her on the registers, the proper cash etiquette and bagging technique. Hannah told me to *make sure Glossy has enough to do*, her words, though I'm not sure what she could have meant by this. There is nothing left to do.

"Another diaper party at my house last night," Glossy says. "I don't know if Precious told you. My sister got herself mixed up with some kind of fitness cult, so her friends and I decided to throw this party to get them to leave her alone." She switches off the Hannah-mandated acoustic guitar playlist. Silence rings through the store. "I think it worked. I got to tell these perfectly toned fitness people that they had to put on a diaper or I wouldn't let them come up to see my sister." The glass doors open and close. "They were all extremely beautiful. I think part of the cult initiation ritual is just eating clarified butter for three straight days. Charlotte said she found herself in a room with two other initiates, braiding their hair. She didn't remember walking into the room. We realized it was some bad shit. The diapers scared them off though. Would you like a bag?"

Someone has brought a suite of hand creams made with chunks of salt from the Dead Sea to the registers. "Ask if they're a member," I say, clicking a playlist called *INSIDE THE CUBE*, the first one I see.

"What would happen if I was a member?" says the customer. Glossy takes a step back.

"There are two types of membership," I begin. The script takes over. "If you're part of the free membership, then for every two hundred dollars you spend you get a ten dollar discount. In the paid membership, which is five dollars a month, you get ten percent off purchases and free shipping within the US." Summer, autumn, winter, spring. A body in motion remains in motion. One two three four five. A body at rest remains at rest.

"Well," says the person, packing their hand cream into a big purse and swiping at their phone, "can you look me up to see if I'm in your system? I come here all the time."

"What's your name?" says Glossy. Three minutes later she's back to telling me about the diaper party, and how she found herself wandering through Sunset Park late that night looking for a place to shit. "Charlotte had locked herself in our bathroom, crying about leaving the cult. I found myself running up and down the block." Someone walks into the store, puts a hand to their brow as though peering into the horizon, and walks out. "The bodega around the corner refused help me out, even though I go there every day. I need to move."

Someone comes in asking to use the bathroom. Glossy shrugs. Someone comes in with a handful of flyers they want us to tape to the store's front window. Someone comes in and asks how long this location has been here. Someone comes in asking for their car keys. Someone comes in and films herself reviewing the store in real time.

"Anyway," says Glossy, "I found a public bathroom. Isn't that wild? Every once in a while you find leftovers of the old socialist ideas they built this town on. Public transit. Bathrooms so you don't shit yourself. It was only after I sat down that I realized I was still wearing a diaper. Could have solved my problem any time."

A man wearing what looks like a bulletproof vest charges into the store. He looks at Glossy, looks at me, looks at the manila envelope in his hand, and then advances to my desk, eyes locked with mine. "Ford Haas," he says.

"Ford isn't here right now," I say, "do you want—"

"You work for Ford Haas."

"He's my owner." I keep accidentally saying this. Glossy gasps.

The man in the vest throws the envelope at my chest and spins around, bolting out of the store. "You are served," he calls as he leaves. It takes a few seconds for me to understand what has happened.

◻ ◻ ◻

Three minutes later a different customer comes in and brings the same Dead Sea hand cream set to the registers. Glossy asks if this person is part of the membership program. The customer would like to know more about the program. "There are two types of membership," I say.

□ □ □

Is it possible that the point of fiction is to dramatize time passing? Or not even dramatize: to bring readers into some purposeful experience of time? You sit down and take as long as it takes to read the words in front of you. A made-up character, a bundle of language, changes over time, and this is how we know time does something to us. Nothing stays in place.

I might say: after the scenes above, time passes. Please put the book down and pick it up some time later.

Weeks Not Months

Calypso, Precious's former clown partner, is getting married. He tells me this in passing: the wedding will happen this very afternoon, in Van Cortlandt Park, and he's invited, but going would mean taking a train and a bus. "An emergency green card wedding," he says, "so it barely counts."

Thirty minutes later Felix and Glossy are crashing through the front door with a bag full of clothing and makeup. They look at us—collapsed on the couch, Precious queuing up another cooking show—as though a fire were burning through the room that we had failed to notice.

"Fucking gerbils," says Glossy.

"Dancing in the park," says Felix. "Beautiful Calypso. Come on."

They struggle to pull Precious out of his pajamas. "Go without me," he says, sinking deeper into the couch. He squirms like a baby when I get too close. "I don't think I can face it."

Felix carries over a palm of stage jewelry and lays each individual piece in a semicircle around Precious's feet. Diamonds producing small rainbows, pearls the size of grapes.

"You're going," Glossy calls over from the bathroom. "You're my invite. I really want to dance."

I know what Precious is going to say the moment before he says it. "How am I supposed to dance with a broken arm," we say together, perfectly synchronized, Precious's eyes locked with mine and widening.

"Listen." Felix lands one arm on Precious's shoulder and one on mine. "I am not going to say *we need this*. But it's possible you need this. It might be good to try getting out of the fucking house."

At the park, we meet Calypso's entire family, every cousin and sibling and uncle in concentric circles around three smoking barbecue pits. Felix takes photos. Someone has twisted off several dozen balloons to look like gigantic roses. A bulldog dives face-first into a bowl of sour cream. Children sweep through the legs of the crowd. Chili and cake, a dozen disposable cameras on the picnic tables waiting to be used.

We arrive in time to catch speeches about the groom. A pink karaoke microphone is passed around. *Evander, what can we say about this guy,* says one of Calypso's uncles. Laughter. *Love is a thing that starts when you don't expect it,* another uncle says. Embarrassed laughter. *Bringing safety to someone's life, real safety, that's an act of love.* Laughter and tears.

The sun bursts through the trees.

"Oh," says Felix. "Right. It's spring."

"Summer basically," says Glossy. The speeches end. We form a line to hug Calypso, and then music starts. The plastic sound made by the little wheels on the disposable cameras clicking forward.

"Emergency wedding," says Calypso. "We couldn't not."

"Beautiful that you could come," says the groom.

"Dancing," says someone.

"Citizenship," says someone else.

"Karaoke."

"I know you. Do I know you?"

A cork flies from a bottle of champagne. "What am I supposed to do now?" says Precious.

"What are you supposed to do?"

"In general. What's the game plan?"

"Listen to this diva. Get out of here, diva."

A bouquet is tossed. I don't see who catches it.

"Grit in the system."

"No, no. Don't start."

"End of the damn world."

"Will we do all this again next year?"

"Absolutely. Oh, absolutely."

We dance.

"Being impossible."

"I know you from somewhere?"

"A rut-shaped rut. I mean rut-sized."

"Need a new job. New place to live."

"Sand in the wheels."

"Full time."

"Expensive. Not cheap."

"Only goes in one direction. That's what I say."

"Diva, angel. Little brother."

"A new life? As in what, start over?"

"What's it called. Guillotines. Those are you?"

"Anyway."

"What's worse?"

□ □ □

"Alright," Ford says as I take a seat between Mora and Hannah. "Alright, we can get started. You may be wondering why I called this meeting. Especially those of you who have been out of the loop, you're probably thinking something awful has happened. When was the last time we were all in the same place? Christmas? Doesn't matter, folks, the point is that I wouldn't call a manager-wide meeting if it wasn't important, though I can assure you right now that nothing terrible has happened, nor is anything bad going to happen. It is important though. Help yourself to a croissant. Here. These are from the bakery by my place. Some of you have been to my place, during happier times. Soon enough I'll have you all over to my place again, where we can eat croissants on my patio. I'll make it a point to set something up, a store-wide dinner party. Some wine. Help yourself. Help yourself. Let's get started." He paces up and down the break room. "Does anyone have any announcements before we get started? Anything anyone wants to get off their chest? No? Hannah, how is the family? No? Alright. So here it is. Some of you may have noticed that the store is in the middle of a few, shall we say, adjustments. There have been a few things shifting around. A few of you may even be carrying around the misguided notions that we are headed downhill as a store. As a family. Because before we even get into it you have to first remember that this is a family affair, folks, some of you I've known for a long time, I've seen my people get married and have kids, alright, and a few of you don't realize it yet but you're with me for the long haul, no matter what happens with this particular brick and mortar store. Let's talk about that. Let's talk about the sister location, the breadwinner of the family. It hasn't been bringing home the bread. It's that simple. And before we even get started, just know that I don't blame you. But where is the bread? Where's it going? Sometimes we've let the sales floor stagnate. It's true. Sometimes here and there I've had to come down and inject a little life into the store, and it wouldn't kill you as I've said repeatedly to post more often to our socials. One social campaign I came up with on the way down here would be called BOOKSTORE DOGS where you get staff to pose with customers' dogs, *here's X or Y staff member with our favorite labradoodle it'll say,* and that way dog owners will feel like they want to come in, they feel welcomed, damn it, because a welcoming family-run store is what sets us apart, it's the one thing we can bring to the neighborhood, it's *service*, folks. Service. But I don't blame you. You shouldn't blame yourselves. I've been in this game a long time, and one thing I've learned is that there's having an idea and then there's acting on it."

The break room, where I prepare coffee in the big urn every morning. There's exactly enough space for the four managers—Hannah, me, Mora, and Joyce in that order—to sit around the oblong table like a jury or chorus as Ford paces around in front of us. The fluorescent ceiling lights, the linoleum floors, everyone's cheekbones and the bags under their eyes. The printed-out photos of December's shoplifter, stuck to the break room fridge with unsellable magnets.

Mora looks at her phone. Hannah drums her fingers on the table. Joyce, I think, is trembling. I take a croissant from the pink box and start ripping it in half, just to also be doing something.

Ford raises his voice. "Let me explain right now that nobody is getting fired. It's not happening. A few things have come to light, it's true, a few things out of my control have transpired, but I think we can react accordingly, get a few pots over the fire, turn this ship around, generate some bread around here. Because, and make no mistake, stores like ours are a dying breed. We owe it to ourselves, and the community owes it to us, damn it, to keep going. There are so few of us left. It used to be you could go to any neighborhood in this city, walk down any block and find a bookstore there, mom-and-pop joints, folks. This is all before your time. We are a dying breed. And those of us left, those of us who haven't died out, we survive because of our ingenuity. Do you realize that? We take risks. Maybe it's not always one hundred percent aboveboard, but we *innovate*, god damn it, we cut our teeth and grow out our fangs and perform social Darwinism in the free marketplace. Yes we do. That's what we've been doing the past nine years, the past five years with the sister location and the extra four with the flagship. This location exists because it innovates. That's what the god damn note-shavers who own this building don't understand. They don't realize that the bookstore invented the free market as we know it. I mean bookstores in general, read a book of history, it isn't the landlords, the extortionists, it's brick-and-mortar, mom-and-pop bookstores holding this system of ours in place, the free market. Do you realize that? I'm telling you. Before bookstores here's what would happen, you would walk into a pharmacy or a grocer and here's what you would see, a man behind a desk, that's it, a man behind a desk. There's no sales floor before the bookstore, no, there's no central promenade where a customer can hold the thing in his hands and see if he wants to purchase it, damn it, before the bookstore the customer has to walk up to the register and ask the young man behind the counter for whatever merchandise the customer wants. Then the bookstore comes along and what happens? Do you know, folks? The bookstore says alright, but you have to let the customer touch the thing first. Innovation! You have to give him a chance to read the first few pages, hold the thing in his hands, see if he likes how it feels, maybe he'll pass that book on to his children, future generations, and suddenly the sales floor is born. It's that simple. Browsing. The customer milling through stock. And that's not all, no, when you create the sales floor everything else changes too, the books themselves need to be beautiful on a sales floor, folks, they have to entice the customer, compete in the free market. The open-plan sales floor creates the maximum amount of freedom for each book to do exactly this, and now we've invented graphic design, industrial design, you name it folks, we've innovated. Innovated! Because when you give the customer the freedom to handle the merchandise, well, he'd better walk up to the register with the best, most expensive merchandise on hand. A million books competing with each other, folks, and the customer lost in the labyrinth of the sales floor, buffeted here and there, attracted to the brightest most colorful book. That's not all. The open sales floor changes the labor force, it changes you, too, folks. Gone are the days of the kid behind the counter fetching your beef cut and eyedrops, no, the open sales floor demands *booksellers*, goddamn it, idealists, college graduates who know their way around a book guiding the customer to the brightest and most expensive one. Closing sales. The landlords don't realize this, they don't see the history, just the next paycheck. It's extortion. What do they know about the free market? We built the system, we have *historical status*, goddamn it, we perform the public service. We deserve some exemption. Some seniority."

He grabs a croissant out of the pink box and stuffs it into his mouth.

"And now the union is crawling up my leg. Now the goddamned union is gumming up the gears in the middle of all this usury with their renewed negotiations and so-called demands. I'm going to let you in on a little secret. You managers, folks, one of your chief responsibilities is to explain to staff that their precious union does not in fact have their best interest at heart. Do I have to spell it out to you? When you make it to manager, you leave the union. And you're better off, aren't you? A substantial raise, a weekly salary. This is by design. Motivation! The same reason we can't have a generation of teenagers flipping burgers and expecting to make twenty-five dollars an hour, goddamn it, folks, it's your job to explain to staff that they have to *earn* it, the profit margin for our store is *slim*. It all has to be accounted for from the very first, and it all goes back into the flagship, God help me. All this accommodation so that the union can have their forty hours per week contract jobs with paid fifteen-minute breaks twice per shift. What does someone on our staff have to complain about? They get to read on the job, they get to buy beautiful merchandise at a discount, they get to interact with the smart educated people who come in looking for X or Y book.

Now the union is saying layoffs will result in a court date. This I do not understand at all, folks, who is saying anything about layoffs? How is it that the union knows, goddamn it, now of all times, when I know none of you talk to the union, how do they know whatever it is they *think they know* about layoffs? Of course it's happening at the same time as everything else, the note-shaving landlords with their complaints and serving papers, not to mention the damage from the grease flood. What am I supposed to do? The union is crawling up my legs so that it can get out from under the floodwater, folks, that's what it is now, and either the union drowns or I will. I shouldn't have to spell it out for you. If I file for bankruptcy, if I go under, if I start breathing grease water instead of air there will be no more jobs to do union bargaining for. That goes for all of you. There is exactly one captain of this ship. If the job creator goes under then you can say goodbye to your job."

A day after the visit from the process server in the bulletproof vest, a second came in and served me another set of papers without removing his motorcycle helmet. Glossy worked that shift too, next to me, behind the registers. The shock of seeing both of us reflected back to ourselves in the visor of the helmet. Later that day we had lunch together—and, seated inside one of the two Thai places down the street with lunch specials starting at twelve dollars, stirring condensed milk and sweet coffee together in my glass, I explained what I knew about the state of the bookstore: everything involving Milton, the store's nonpayment of rent, our frozen accounts with every major distributor. I also explained that Ford had threatened in an email to fire as many people as he could to cut costs. I said if she stayed on staff for another three weeks Glossy would get a seventy-five cent pay increase and membership in the union, which would make her much harder to fire. She said nobody told her.

"So this is where we are," Ford says. "Layoffs will have me in court with the union, and the landlords have me in court for back rent. The flagship has enough used stock coming in to stay open, to weather us through this storm, God help me, but you folks, the sister location, you have to know we can't stay open if we're not selling merchandise, which I cannot afford to keep buying. So here's what we're going to do. We're taking a pause. You take the week off. It's on me. You take the week off, and in return you're going to tell staff there just aren't any hours this week. We just do not have the hours, Hannah, folks, you're simply unable to schedule their hours, whatever you need to say. No one is getting fired, but we need to take this pause. I'm going to figure something out. The lights will stay on, but the doors will be closed. I'll be here, figuring something out. Maybe I'll call on one or two of you to come in and we'll work something out together, maybe we'll keep the doors open for customers, our loyal customers, in case some business comes our way. We can carry all of the downstairs merchandise into the main sales floor, show off our beautiful children's toys and feather lamps. Online orders will stay up as always. That means shipping." He looks at me. "So that's a good idea. Be on the lookout, keep an eye on your phone, folks, because I may end up calling you, but for the sake of simplicity let's just say this coming week will constitute a pause, a week off, on me. The doors will stay closed, or they won't. We'll screen for customers at the door so no more god damn opportunists can come in serving papers. We'll keep overhead low. I'll figure something out."

□ □ □

Last night Precious and I opened a bottle of moonshine and watched *Chopped Junior* until dawn. This wasn't something we had planned—I came home and he said he was getting food delivered, and by the time our order arrived the second episode had automatically begun playing, and then we were caught in its cycle. Now it's the following day. The sun roams around. We move from video to video. We watch a clip of Precious's favorite internet chef preparing kimchi in a bright kitchen. I close my eyes to better concentrate on the slow sound of hands worrying liquid from a cabbage. When I wake up Precious is watching a video demonstration of how to forage for scallions outside the replica medieval castle at the very top of Fort Tryon Park. I look out the window and catch the blue reflection of his TV. I suppose another few hours pass. The internet chef chops scallions on a cutting board shaped like a fish.

Felix and I went to Fort Tryon Park once. We wandered through the herb garden behind the castle, noting the placards that indicated pomegranate flower for witches, rue for poison, rosemary for the worms that burrow through teeth. What I remember clearest was the smell: stones reverberating their cold against stained glass, old tapestries, and the wooden ceiling. Paintings. Felix found a temptation scene with multiple conjoined demons taking the shape of a rooster licking Christ with a big tongue coming out of its collective vulva. She has since repurposed this vignette into a tattoo design; it's famous.

Felix is on tour. She bought plane tickets to Philadelphia, Chicago, Minneapolis, and Seattle for three days each, then posted her dates in each city online. Immediately her schedule filled. She keeps an Excel sheet for appointments now, freelancing, doing her guillotines. A guillotine artist. I fall asleep and dream about peeing in a corner behind the TV, then in a cast iron pot over a high flame on one of the cooking shows. I wake up and reach for my crotch to make sure I didn't actually pee.

Here's what happened with Felix. While she was in Los Angeles tattooing the internet celebrity's butt, she *got frustrated with the situation as a whole* (her words) and switched up her formula, bringing the guillotine's blade all the way down and throwing in a meticulously rendered likeness of the celebrity's head rolling out from under the stocks, trailing blood, eyes crossed and tongue out. The decapitated head made the celebrity furious. He posted a barrage of thirty-second videos denouncing Felix, five minutes in total. This only made her more famous. Now she's everywhere.

Felix. When I came home yesterday Precious was already watching *Chopped Junior.* "This one is really good," he said. "The contestants are children, but it's still a humiliating deathmatch, but they're twelve years old so they're incapable of not fucking up. Look at this kid, he's burning his onions." We watched a child attempt to open a jar of apricot marmalade, his face purpling. "I could kick these kids' asses at this," said Precious. "Maybe he'll cry."

Now a full day has passed. I keep my phone close in case Ford calls. Precious brings over a plate of dried sausage and pickled eggs. When I look out the window, it's red. *The energy in the kitchen is very, like, pow,* says one of the children.

I learn that every episode is identical. The secret ingredient is always candy. The children, reading from cue cards, explain their decision-making process in incorporating gummy worms with salmon tartare. They repeat the footage of whatever dramatic moment has just occurred—a pan burnt, a finger cut, an ingredient missing—at least twice. The celebrity guest always has the nicest thing to say about every dish. Meghan Markle, Tony Hawk. And the completed dishes, finally, get a maximum of two seconds of screen time each. "Looks like shit," says Precious, every time.

And Felix? Does she get home soon? Do the particles of sand finally eat her? Or what?

◻ ◻ ◻

Several hours later, when we are both drunk, Precious tells me about the guest house on his grandmother's multi-acre plot of land, a former dairy farm. "Enough space to cultivate honeybees," he says.

"Make mead. Or grow mushrooms. Enough space to raise some goats and make cheese. There are these huge vats in the basement we could use to brew beer. Distill vodka, or whatever, gin. Anything we want. A sustainable farm. Nonexistent cost of living." His eyes survey the room. We almost make eye contact. "If we got a bunch of people out there. A commune. We would need a critical mass."

He waves his hand, dismissing what he has just said. "Anyway, anyway. You know."

□ □ □

I read, and am taken by an experience of open vertigo at the fact that I can understand any of the words in front of me. They turn into music. I read in my bed on its shipping pallet, my bed next to the window overlooking the aboveground train coming now to a screeching halt, white sparks raining down on the dark block for fractions of a second. The ink on a page becomes a group of people in a room talking. It becomes a skyscraper turned to rubble, the ocean at sunrise. Nothing changes when I put the book down. I stare at the ceiling, fall asleep until midnight and wake with my finger between pages, lights on. I read and synapses fire, whatever happens in my brain happens and I speak to the dead.

I read books that seem to contain everything in them. Books that are cities, ant colonies where each ant is a word, books that seem both to exist and iterate existence. And then I read books like sheer drapery, a gossamer, a barely there.

Most nights a catch in my attention forms. A sinkhole around which I drift, reading. Sinking deeper into bed. I encounter the word *sidereal* and have to sound it out several times—*side-ear-y-ull*—before I look up a definition. Related to distant stars. Elsewhere the phrase *a rain of parallel bright lines across the rafters* catches me. The centripetal force of the sinkhole dictates its turn, and the parallel lines across rafters become lines tracing the progress of stars, and I begin to wonder how it could be possible that the author knew that I had just been dreaming about stars, just now before waking up, caught in the fugue that passes between reading, sleeping, and waking up in order to resume reading. How is it that a written and printed book could possibly transmit information regarding events that have yet to occur, I wonder, supine in bed, events such as my early shift tomorrow, which I seem to be reading about now, and the particular flavor of panic or exhaustion that will set in at about ten in the morning and not melt off until I have crawled back into bed with this same book in front of me, this book in my hands now falling with my wrist onto my chest, now in front of my face again repeating the thing about the rafters, still at the parallel lines across rafters. I turn and turn on the book's axis, my eyes tracing ink.

I fall asleep and wake up to the sound of sawing.

Final Ten Notes about Work

1.

The sister location closes. Ford moves me back to the flagship.

Arthur is singing. I knife open a Simon and Schuster box and tear out its invoice. Cold light, metal shelves, packing tape lining the frayed edges of two standing desks. Dima paces in and out of the receiving room, shooting glances in my direction and looking away. He files a cigarette behind his ear. Over the sound of Arthur singing, I can hear Ford explaining something to Mora and Hannah on the sales floor. "A different protocol, folks," I think he says.

And all the books I never got around to stealing—books that seem alien to me now, almost hostile, in their buildup of time during my absence—remain piled on the shelf behind my computer, my old secret spot.

2.

Here's what happened. When it became clear that Ford couldn't talk his landlords out of demanding back rent, he started an online charity-type fundraiser for the sister location's continued existence. Crucially, though, right as the person who runs the store's Amazon account was about to press publish on his thing, Ford changed the campaign page's phrasing to include the word *loan*. A small loan for a small business. Contribute now. Why did he do this? None of us know.

The terms of the loan, written at the bottom of the fundraiser page in Ford's manic prose, laid out bimonthly payments and varying interest rates, sliding scale plans suggesting multiple tiers of investment. *Public servant tier, savant tier, angel tier.* Hannah read the whole campaign aloud during an emergency mid-shift happy hour break. A third of the way through it became clear that Ford had been wrapping his head around his scheme in real time as he wrote. "This is literally fraud," said Hannah. The image of a feral possum burst fully formed into my head. Its little teeth and nose. A clawing-animal impulse that locks into place and becomes permanent—a long empty tunnel with debt repayment at the other end. Sitting there, at the bar, in the middle of the day, I experienced for the first time what must have been a pang of sympathy for Ford, his whole mode of being. "We're fucked," was all Hannah would say between whiskey sours.

The neighborhood's donors transformed into investors with the expectation of return. The circle of attention widened. The public took interest in the loan's terms and began to seed. The blue line at the top of the campaign page kept growing. In a matter of weeks it filled entirely.

3.

"No amount of money is enough," says Ford. "There's no ceiling, only floor." He tells me this as we clear half-empty sister location shelves (History, Sociology, Gender Studies) to make room for an array of Beanie Baby-type plush dolls he wants sold by the end of the day. A few blocks south from us there is a toy store where, on trash days, freelancers will rip into the black plastic bags left on the curb in order to salvage officially unsellable stock. The dolls' massive wide-set eyes gloss over the sales floor. "What I need is more time, folks, more time," Ford says.

The shoplifter returns, making off with a dozen or so vegan leather purses before anyone notices.

This is all several weeks ago now—I don't know why I use present tense. Some moments from the past I experience continuously. Most of it washes over me, leaving behind a kind of scum, a milk skin.

Customers start asking questions about the loan that no one can answer. Glossy manages to twist placating non-responses out of these interactions, but more credulous members of staff tend to call over a manager, standing wide-eyed behind me or Hannah or Mora as we explain how impossible it is to know how anything is to be done. It doesn't take long for the public's bafflement and concern to congeal into rage. "I want my money back," says everyone.

4.

"People may turn up," says Ford. "Some people, I don't know who exactly, they might come in and ask for me, folks. I'm not saying this will happen, but it might. What I need you to know, what I need everyone to remember right now, is that I'm out of town. I'm vacationing. Right? I'm with my family in the Adirondacks. We do this every year. The weather's getting warm, and what we do every year around when it starts getting warm is we go stay in a cabin in the Adirondacks. The cabin belongs to a family friend. I don't even know the address! My wife knows. Very remote. No internet, no cell service, folks, nothing but family time and maybe a good book. Alright? Is everyone clear? I need you to look at me. If they ask for money, you don't have to give them anything. Legally. If anyone comes in here and starts making threats, well, that's what the police are for. So tell me. Where do you say I am when people start coming into the store asking for me?"

5.

Someone from the union shows up with two stacks of leaflets and a box of donuts. The first stack, done in thick serif font over asymmetrical red blocks, describes the various lines of support offered by the union to staff workers who believe they've been asked to do something illegal. Hannah carries this stack in one arm and the box of donuts in the other down to the break room, creating a little shrine to staff on the oblong table. The second group of leaflets she deposits in the paper recycling bin downstairs, buried under the day's cardboard. I find a stray page several hours later: a ream of anonymous, Times New Roman printouts explaining why and how to conduct a wildcat strike. I take a photo of one of these tracts and text it to Glossy.

Precious shows up with three homemade bento boxes. The day warms just enough to sit on the perimeter of the dog park adjacent the natural history museum and eat. "Which one are you?" says Precious, pointing to a shifting huddle of dogs.

Milton is the last to show up. I watch his minivan inch behind Antoine's truck just as the store's phone rings and Hannah does her full *thank you for calling Book Buffet, this is Hannah speaking, how may I help you?* routine though she knows it's Ford on the other end. You can see his name on the little screen. I have opened my hand truck and am wheeling it outside when I hear Hannah ask *who is Milton?*

Milton perches on the corner, smoking his Camels. It looks like he's switched to menthol. He gestures at his minivan, an unreflecting silver, stuffed full of sci-fi paperbacks that fell off the truck of a warehouse somewhere outside Philadelphia. My back produces a full symphonic arrangement of pain, from the outside part of my butt all the way up the neck's hinge into the skull. "Alright then boss," says Milton. When I return inside, jamming a small mountain of boxes through the front door and grunting under the weight, I see Hannah holding the phone out to me, receiver first.

"Milton," Ford screams when I get the phone to my ear. It sounds like he has been speaking uninterrupted this whole time.

"Hello," I say.

"Milton should be coming by with some stuff. What we need to do is this, folks, return like we've never returned before. The biggest return in the history of our business, goddamn it, make their heads spin. Milton's stuff will give you a running start but don't stop there. Return it all, folks. We need all the credit we can get. Prune the tree. The whole store. Shut down for the day if you have to. Take an afternoon, get all hands on it. Scanning, scanning. Pack it up."

"How are the Adirondacks?" I say, but he has already hung up.

6.

This is taking too long—I'm out of time. What happened was that we emptied the store of almost all its contents, returning every book we could find to its respective distributor's warehouse in order to be pulped. Mora, Hannah, and I scanned while Joyce and the remaining staff members carried kids' books upstairs, consolidating the entire sales floor into a dense central nucleus. We worked with the lights off, on our knees, scanning. Takeout boxes on the floor, everyone with their own pair of headphones wedged in their ears. This took three days. On the fourth day the fire marshal came and chained the front door shut.

I was still on the subway when Hannah texted. *Don't bother coming in*, she said. *It's done.*

"You have five minutes to collect whatever you can carry," the fire marshal had apparently said, swinging the silver chain around in one hand and the big padlock in the other.

7.

Now I'm here again.

Dima taps me on the shoulder. "Lunch," he says. When I turn around there's Felix, standing there, in the receiving room, framed in garbage bags and boxes. She smells like charcoal, and hands me a bunch of paper tulips it looks like she folded by hand.

"A familiar scene," she says.

I try smelling the tulips. They smell like the hand soap in Felix's apartment.

"Ouroboros," I say.

"A frictionless space."

Dima pretends to yawn, then pretends to spit.

We walk to a diner several blocks south, settling into our seats as a pot of coffee is waved in the air between our heads. "I'm not a hundred percent sure I can afford to eat out anymore," I say.

"What's your biggest sandwich?" Felix asks the server, who is still filling our cups with red coffee. "We'll split something."

"Tuna melt," the server says. "Very massive."

"We'll have one please," she says.

We sit for a while in silence.

Her face. It looks different.

"In Minneapolis I had a thought," she says. "Related to money, actually. Right now I make more tattooing than I ever will at the gallery. It's still not a lot, but I'm internet famous, so that's something." She shifts around in her chair. "Tattooing seems like the thing for me. Going around wherever there's demand. Getting better. Digging. I don't need to shut myself up in a room making high-concept shit no one will see. I don't need to be validated as a *serious artist.* It took time but I learned this about myself. A piece on someone's leg is actually better than a painting belonging to some rich person. Don't you think?" She says all this slowly, each word a soft piece of clay in need of forming. This image lingers, Felix shaping clay, dough in her hands. I have a hard time keeping track of what she's actually saying.

"Tuna melt," says the server, sliding an open-faced sandwich onto the table.

The cheese glistens in the low light. "This is like three cans of tuna," says Felix. We take turns trying to cut it in half—folds of meat pouring over wet bread—before Felix starts in again, as slowly as before. "I was wondering if you would take care of Girlfriend for a bit. If I tour for a couple months I'll be set for the rest of the year." She lifts a glob of fish to her mouth. "No one knows her like you, other than Precious, but lately he seems a little . . ." She waves her hand. "Anyway you don't have to answer right now. You could live in my room if you want. For as long as I'm gone. We'd figure something out." Her stare comes at a long angle. Then, "god," she says, "this sandwich is awful."

When I bite into it, I taste the mash of several pasted-together carcasses and mayonnaise. It could be anything. Felix and I look at each other. Wet pulp cooling against a spring day. *A world full of blood diamonds,* I suddenly think, but don't say.

The sun tears through the diner's windows.

"How many animals died so we could eat this slimy-ass thing. Let alone this cheese." She holds her hands up. "Not excelsior," she says. "Not excelsior! I think that's it for me. I think I'm done."

8.

I walk Felix to the subway and return to the flagship.

After the fire marshal chained the sister location doors, Hannah arranged for all managers and remaining staff to meet in Ford's office in order to apprehend a straight answer from him regarding future employment. He beckoned us inside, the look on his face bordering something close to euphoria. "Unforeseeable," he said, beaming. "We're frustrated, of course. Livid, even. But we managed to squeak by, folks. It's all behind us. We're moving forward."

I don't really remember what happened. Hannah purpled. The air in the room swept into and then back out of Ford's two lungs. "No one is getting fired," he said. "No illegal dealings. Let me make that perfectly clear. We will have to shuffle some things around. But we move forward. You will be receiving new contracts. And Hannah, folks, Hannah, you and I need to talk about your staff members and the goddamned union. Some other time, but immediately, as soon as possible. After this. The good news is that everyone gets a promotion. I've figured that one out at least. The union doesn't need to get involved."

Over the next seven days, Ford promoted all the sister location staff members, including Glossy, to manager, with a regular salary of $500 per week before tax. Every day we gained a manager, until there was no one left to promote. No one knew how anything worked.

A few days of this, and then Ford summoned everyone he had just promoted into his office, all in one meeting. I wasn't there. But Glossy texted me as it was happening: *who even is this bitch*, she said.

> *his head really is so big*
> *watch him run for mayor or something*
> *wait I'm fired*
> *oh we're all fired hahaha*
> *jesus*

I thought about the strike pamphlets discarded by Hannah. When you're promoted to manager, you leave the union—this strips you of any contract, protection, organizational leverage. I still don't entirely understand how it all works.

9.

Now what? In the receiving room Dima listens to Rachmaninoff on full blast, throwing boxes to the top of an eight-foot pile. The remaining sister location managers trail their respective doubles around the shop, gathering intelligence. I follow Dima's lead and stack. Maybe the plan is for Ford to assess which of the two identical managers he wants to keep, and fire the other. Maybe it's all an elaborate job interview, this burlesque.

"Aye captain," Dima says when I suggest we do anything.

"You're the boss," I tell him as we clamber up to the roof for a smoke break.

"Glad I wasn't fired," says Arthur, to no one. Arthur being the union's sole surviving member.

Probably this is what will happen. Dima is better than me—stronger, faster, more fluent with the point-of-sale and inventory software—so I'll be fired, and so will Joyce and possibly Mora. Hannah will keep her job if she doesn't quit. The flagship will churn through its laborers, remaining ultimately the same. Ford will smear his way through whatever set of lawsuits come next, or he'll file for bankruptcy. All this does happen. All this and much more. I imagine myself several years from now, finding myself in the old neighborhood and dropping into the sister location, which has a different name but is back up and running, owned by someone else. The walls have been painted red and the desk next to the registers where shipping and receiving once happened has been replaced with what looks like a present-wrapping station. The customers browsing the rows of candles and adult coloring books all seem younger than they used to. One of the city's ubiquitous auburn poodles throws its front legs onto the registers in obvious anticipation of the treat that emerges from the hands of the staff worker, someone I don't recognize, and lands into the dog's open mouth. I drift into Fiction and see all the same books as before. *Maybe they're literally the same books*, I think, running a finger over their spines—though I boxed those books up myself, I hauled them with Antoine from the sales floor into his UPS truck, lifting each box one at a time with my back. I watched him drive them away. Still, maybe those same books made it all the way back to their respective warehouses, only to be resold at a 35–46 percent discount to this new bookstore—the same bookstore, only different—where they once again sit, unsold, as a constellation of hand-knit gloves and ethical baby toys orbits around them. I pick up a novella I've never seen before and read the entire thing in the store's corner, realizing only as I look up again that the sun has set and the staff prepares the night's close. They close earlier than we did.

The year is 2022. Precious, I imagine, sips homemade milk punch from an estate sale glass. The glass probably has some dead person's graduation photo on it, the milk punch a cloudy rose.

Glossy I imagine downtown, just beginning her night shift at a free clinic or an emergency room, gasping with delight when a coworker compliments the guillotine tattoo on her clavicle, right across from the one that says *WHAT IS TO BE DONE?*

I imagine Felix staring into Girlfriend's tank. I imagine Girlfriend scanning Felix's smell with her doubled tongue, searching. She smells like ginger. In an ideal world I walk out of the bookstore and in the direction of wherever they are.

10.

The calamity has already occurred. History keeps ending and ending. I walk to a pizza place down the street and write all this down. On the big TV they play college football. I pour from the wrong end of the shaker, depositing a thick carpet of red pepper flakes onto my slice of pizza. I shiver in my coat, bones against flesh. Somewhere it's morning. And somewhere else a tropical storm builds force until it's reclassified as a hurricane.

Acknowledgments

The convention of giving a novel too many titles I have taken from Clarice Lispector's *The Hour of the Star*. The phrase "a bright beadlike row of unaffiliated moments" is from Nicholson Baker's *The Mezzanine*. "An expert in something that is unnecessary" and "the situation is more dire still" are both from David Graeber's *Bullshit Jobs*. "The World's Got Everything in It" is the name of a song by Mince Meat.

Thank you to everyone at the University of Nebraska Press and Zero Street Fiction: the endlessly supportive Timothy Schaffert; Courtney Ochsner; Kasey Peters, who plucked this book from the slush pile; SJ Sindu; Katrina Vassallo; Lacey Losh; Lindsey Welch; Rebecca Jefferson; Sarah Kee; Tish Fobben; and the memory of Barbara DiBernard.

I'm extremely grateful to the Anderson Center at Tower View for giving me time and space to work on this project. Thank you Adam Wiltgen, Stephanie Rogers, and the rest of the Anderson Center staff for your support.

To Corley Miller, Sarah Yanni, Aditi Kini, Effy Morris, David Connor, Phuong T. Vuong, Easton Smith, and all members of Shadow Shop and Twenty Lines (Hannah Rubin, Lucy Blagg, Kyra

Lunenfeld, Maggie Lange, among others), who advocated for this work in its early stages. Thank you to the infinitely patient Brian Evenson, Jess Arndt, Douglas Kearney, Anthony McCann, Tisa Bryant, Lily Hoang, and Kate Zambreno, whose mentorship has been like a skeleton key. The luminaries Julio Neijens, Andrew Plimpton, Kenneth Reveiz, Jess Goldschmidt, Mathew Weitman, Gray Lamb, and Emily Bannon. Mom, Pop, Adena, Paul, thank you.

This book would not exist without Jhani Randhawa, Erik Abrahams, Kelly Gilbert, and my friends in the receiving room and on the sales floor, who know who they are. Thanks aren't enough.

IN THE ZERO STREET FICTION SERIES

All Daughters Are Awesome Everywhere: Stories
by DeMisty D. Bellinger

Slow Guillotine
by Teo Rivera-Dundas

I Make Envy on Your Disco
by Eric Schnall

Daddy Issues: Stories
by Eric C. Wat

Forget I Told You This
by Hilary Zaid

www.ingramcontent.com/pod-product-compliance
Lightning Source LLC
Chambersburg PA
CBHW030321020726
47493CB00004B/1114